Lori suddenly knew what she would do. She would treat all of her friends—Elaine, Alex, *and* Kit—to a vacation in Hawaii. It had been months since they had seen one another, and this would be a *perfect* way for all of them to get together. A whole week in Hawaii, with her very best friends! With all the good modeling jobs she'd had lately, even three more plane tickets wouldn't be hard to manage.

"I have a great idea," Lori said to Kit, struggling to contain her excitement. "Let's *all* go to Hawaii!"

Kit stared at Lori, her eyes growing large and round. "It's a terrific idea, Lori. But even if the condo is free, I can't afford the plane ticket, and I don't think Alex and Elaine can, either."

"But *I* can!" Lori jumped up, ran around the table, and threw her arms around Kit's neck. "I can, and I *want* to! It will be my Christmas present to everybody! The best Christmas we've ever had!"

HAWAIIAN CHRISTMAS
created by Eileen Goudge

Published by
Dell Publishing Co., Inc.
1 Dag Hammarskjold Plaza
New York, New York 10017

Created by Cloverdale Press
133 Fifth Avenue
New York, New York 10003

Cover photo by Pat Hill

Laurel-Leaf Library ® TM 766734,
Dell Publishing Co., Inc.

Super Seniors™ is a trademark of Dell Publishing
Co., Inc.,
New York, New York.

ISBN: 0-440-93649-7

RL: 5.8

Printed in the United States of America

December 1986

10 9 8 7 6 5 4 3 2 1

WFH

Chapter One

"Turn to your left, Lori," Bruce said, snapping the shutter. "Head back, arm over your head. Now turn, keep on turning." His voice was almost a whisper as he gave Lori directions and took picture after picture. "That's it. Great. Now, come toward me. Keep coming."

Lori Woodhouse licked her lips and lifted her arm over her head, eyes half-shut against the glare of the bright lights, swinging slightly to one side so that the camera could pick up the sheen of her long, golden hair. She took two slow steps toward the photographer, her lips parted slightly. The black-sequined evening gown she was modeling clung to her so tightly she was having trouble breathing, and she hoped she wasn't perspiring so heavily that it showed on camera.

She held the pose a moment, then turned and gave the photographer a slow, provocative smile. Modeling was very much like act-

1

ing, Lori's agent had told her when she first came to New York. Right now she was shooting a perfume advertisement, and to look seductive in the photographs she had to play a seductive role for the camera.

"Hey, Lori, telephone call," one of Bruce's assistants called out from behind the lights.

Bruce straightened up and ran a hand through his dark curls. "It's time for a break, anyway," he said, with satisfaction. "You're doing great, Lori. Just hold on to that mood. When we come back, I want to shoot you on the sofa."

Lori giggled as she hiked up her evening gown and hurried toward the telephone in the corner of the studio, her heels clicking against the hard wood floor. *Shoot you on the sofa.* The kids back home in Glenwood would laugh if they could see her now.

At the thought of Glenwood and her friends, Lori felt a twinge of homesickness. A year ago, when she was in the middle of her senior year at Glenwood High, she never would have thought her dream of being a fashion model would come true so quickly, so completely. Here she was just five short months after graduation, living in New York and working for CHIC, one of the most prominent agencies in the city, modeling designer clothes and products and living what her friends would call a glamorous life.

Lori took the receiver the assistant held out to her. "Hello," she said.

"Lori, this is Clare Karlysle. I'm sorry to interrupt you in the middle of a shoot, but it's important. I'd like to see you today. Could you stop by the office when you're finished working?"

"Sure," Lori said, swallowing her surprise. Clare Karlysle, the head of CHIC, had a reputation for being extremely hardworking. She didn't usually take time out to talk directly with the models, but for some reason, she had taken a special interest in Lori's career. She was responsible for Lori getting some terrific assignments lately and Lori knew she owed a lot to Clare. "I'll come just as soon as I can," she added, glancing at the studio clock. "We should be through here in another hour."

"That's fine," Clare said. "I may be in a meeting, but I'll leave instructions for my secretary to interrupt me when you get here." She paused. "Oh, and Lori, don't worry. This is good news — you're not being called on the carpet."

It had been an odd series of accidents that had brought Lori to New York to work for CHIC. She had come at Clare Karlysle's personal invitation, after Lou Shapiro, a photographer and a friend of Chris Farleigh, had given her Lori's portfolio. Lori's insides still turned upside down when she thought of Chris Farleigh. Even though Chris had been much older than Lori, they had become very close last year, and she had hoped that they might get even closer.

But it wasn't meant to be. Their lives had taken different directions, and now she rarely heard from him. But it was because of Chris that she'd had a chance to establish herself in New York, and she knew she'd never forget him. Down deep, part of her still loved him.

"Okay, Lori," Bruce called, setting up another camera. "Are you ready to get back to work?"

The assistant, a young girl not much older than Lori, looked at her enviously. "Work? Looks more like play to me."

Lori frowned thoughtfully as she walked toward the sofa, thinking about what Bruce's assistant had said. Lounging on a cream-colored velvet sofa, looking beautiful for the camera. It's true—it didn't seem much like work. *But it is*, she thought, arranging herself on the sofa, her gown pulled up to reveal one long, tanned leg. She was getting paid for it, and getting paid at a fabulous rate. She tossed her hair back, offering Bruce a slow, sexy smile as he came in for a close shot. She had everything she'd ever wanted. She should be completely, deliriously happy.

Why *wasn't* she?

"Taxi!" The November sky was leaden and gray, and a near-freezing drizzle made the streets shiny and slick, awash with waves of honking yellow cabs and rumbling buses. Lori stamped her feet in their suede boots and clutched her fur jacket tighter around her neck to keep warm as she held up a gloved hand and signaled for a cab. When one finally pulled up at the curb in front of her, she climbed in and gave the driver the agency's Madison Avenue address. Shutting her eyes, she settled back in the seat as the driver pulled into the traffic-clogged streets with a jerk and made a quick right turn off Second Avenue to head west.

She couldn't stop thinking about the question that had popped into her mind back in the studio. Here she was, a rising young model with what looked like a terrific career ahead of her. She had a great apartment in Greenwich Village with her best friend, Kit, and lots of good-looking guys to go out with on the weekends. In fact, she went out *every* weekend, to dinner, to shows, to the ballet. To an outsider, it must seem that she had everything.

She shook her head. She couldn't understand why she felt such dissatisfaction? Why did she feel that there ought to be something more to life than standing in front of a camera looking beautiful, or dressing up to go out and have a good time? Why couldn't she simply accept the wonderful things that were happening to her, the way the other models at the agency did, and stop asking herself so many questions?

Lori sighed. The trouble was that she'd never been able to avoid difficult questions. Of course, modeling wasn't the piece of cake that most people thought it was. Was *that* what was bothering her? There were plenty of difficult things about it, and every model complained from time to time. Nobody really *liked* posing for six straight hours under hot lights, or being yelled at by cantankerous photographers, or getting stuck with pins by frenzied assistants. And being posed out of doors in a bathing suit the week before Thanksgiving certainly wasn't fun. Modeling wasn't entirely the glamorous job it had seemed to be when she was back in Glenwood, dreaming about life in the big city, where exciting things happened in a hurry.

Lori opened her eyes and braced herself as the taxi made a two-wheeled turn onto Fifth Avenue and squealed to a stop for a red light in front of Saks, its Christmas windows glowing like jewels against the afternoon's gray drizzle. No, she had to admit that it wasn't the modeling work that bothered her so much. It was the life she was living that really troubled her. Sometimes she sensed that it was moving along *too* fast. She was left feeling like one of the mannequins in the Saks window, dressed in a high-fashion outfit and made up to look sexy and sophisticated, but inside, empty and hollow. Worse than that, most of the time she felt insecure and more than a little bit lost as the big city whirled and danced around her, glittering and glamorous.

At the next corner, a group of art students from the nearby Art Institute clustered at the curb, waiting for the light to change, huge portfolios under their arms. Lori looked at them with a sudden longing. She had always loved to draw and at one time even thought of a career in art. Now, after a long day of modeling, she often sat down with her sketch pad to draw or put up her easel in front of the north window to paint. She wondered if she could find the time to take some courses, find out if she had any talent, and fulfill the other half of her dream.

Lori shook her head, trying to shake the crazy thoughts from her head. She was doing what she wanted to do—wasn't she? Why should she get such crazy notions? She thought of how she felt when she painted or drew and knew that she couldn't deny that her artwork was far more rewarding than her modeling. Drawing never left her feeling bored or frustrated—or empty.

She looked back at the students as the taxi pulled away. Maybe she should *make* time for classes at the institute. If she cut back on the number of jobs she took, she could do it. It would mean that she would make less money, but that wouldn't be a problem, since she already had more money saved than she knew what to do with. And as far as Lori was concerned, doing what you *wanted* to do was far more important than making money. She decided she would enroll in the institute next semester. Even if she didn't have any special talent, at least she would be doing something that she loved.

"It's so good to see you, Lori," Clare Karlysle said enthusiastically, coming around her large glass-topped desk. She put her hands on Lori's shoulders and looked at her, smiling warmly. The faint floral scent of her perfume wafted around them. "I hear such wonderful things from the photographers who work with you. They all tell me that in addition to being naturally photogenic, you have a natural talent for movement." She turned and picked up a folder from her desk. "Believe me, that kind of talent makes it much easier for a photographer to do his best work."

"Thanks," Lori said shyly, letting Clare lead her toward the sofa. The executive suite of CHIC reflected its director's style: sleek and elegant and up-to-the-minute, done in monochromatic beiges with plenty of glass and chrome and accents of red and blue. The sofa was piled high with cushions, and Lori sank down into it, feeling overwhelmed by her surroundings. Clare sat down in a chair beside the sofa and straightened the bow of her ivory-colored tailored blouse.

"Have some very exciting news for you, Lori," she said, opening the folder and pushing her glasses up on top of her dark hair. "There's a terrific opportunity coming your way."

"Wow. Great," Lori said, trying to match Clare's enthusiasm. "What is it?"

"I've been working with the marketing director at Cachet Cosmetics. They're getting ready to launch a new line, and they're looking for a fresh face, someone young and versatile, who can handle all kinds of looks. The promotion will be a big one. It will mean a one-year contract for the model, at a salary that dazzles even me—and her face will appear in every major magazine in the country. It's wonderful exposure for the face they select." She leaned forward. "Cachet has studied your portfolio, Lori. They've decided it's *your* face they want."

Lori sat up, stunned. "Me?" Her voice squeaked in surprise. "But I . . . I can't . . . ."

Clare laughed softly. "Of course you can, my dear," she said. "Why, this is the kind of stuff that dreams are made of! It's a great deal of work, of course, but a big assignment like this at the beginning of your career is a *wonderful* opportunity. Your face will be known all over the country. Cachet is willing to invest a great deal of time and money in you. It's a chance you can't possibly turn down."

Lori looked down at her hands, remembering what she had decided in the taxi. She couldn't set aside the time to study art if she accepted this kind of long-term assignment. It was only fair to let Clare know what she was considering. "I . . . I've been thinking about a lot of things, Clare," she began. "I've decided that I want to spend some time studying art. I'm going to take courses at the Art Institute as soon as the new semester begins."

Clare looked puzzled. "Art courses? But why?"

"Because I'm interested in art, and I've always wanted to study painting," Lori said, shifting uncomfortably.

"But your career isn't *in* art," Clare said, getting up and going to the window. "I mean, you may like to draw or paint, but you have a natural talent for modeling, and that's where you need to devote your energy."

"But—" Lori began.

"Oh, I know, dear," Clare interrupted. She turned to Lori, her voice sympathetic. "I know that sometimes the work is very hard. The long hours, the lights, the changes, the level of tension and anxiety. Sometimes it all seems like too much, especially in the beginning, when you're first getting started. And believe me, plenty of the best-known models have thought about leaving modeling for something less demanding at one time or another." She paused. "But they change their minds the minute an important job comes along, because they recognize that's what they really ought to be doing, that's where the challenges lie."

"Yes, but, I really *want* to study art," Lori said, feeling stubborn. "And I'm sure that Cachet can find another face that will do just as well."

Clare came toward her. "It's *your* face Cachet wants, my dear," she said, her voice a little cooler. "I've told them a great deal about you, and they're utterly determined to have

11

you." She smiled, but Lori thought that her eyes looked hard and remote. "You know, of course, how strongly CHIC has backed you up to now. Perhaps I need to remind you that this job is a plum not only for you but for CHIC, as well. I'm delighted that Cachet came to me to help them find exactly what they were looking for—and I'm pleased to be able to have what they need."

Lori nodded. She understood what Clare was saying. The agency had done a lot for her, had helped her get jobs that few beginners had a chance at. The Cachet work meant a good commission for Clare, as well as a terrific salary for Lori. And in a way, Clare's reputation was on the line here, since she had sold Cachet on Lori as a model for their new line. If she couldn't deliver, she might lose Cachet's business for the agency altogether. Lori swallowed, feeling trapped. She *was* grateful to Clare for everything she had done to help her get started in her modelling career. But did that mean that she had to give up what she wanted to do?

"You know, Lori, I think I understand what's the matter," Clare said, in a softer voice, sitting on the sofa next to Lori. "You've been working awfully hard lately, running from one job to another. You must be exhausted. The idea of another job, especially a long-term contract, must be overwhelming right now." She smiled. "What you need is a vacation!"

"A vacation?" Lori looked out the window at the gray sky that hung over the city. The freezing drizzle had turned to sleet, and just looking at it made her shiver.

"Of course!" Clare put her hand on Lori's arm. "You need to get away from this glum New York winter to a place where the sun shines and there are beaches and flowers and dancing and handsome young men! You've been working too hard, that's all, and you're tired."

Lori hesitated. "It would be nice to get away from the city for a while," she admitted, "but I don't think I could . . . ."

"Of *course* you could!" Clare laughed delightedly. "And I know just the place, my dear! I have a condo on Maui, and it's free for the Christmas holiday. A wonderful, relaxing Hawaiian vacation is exactly what you need to help you set your priorities straight again! You'll have plenty of time to rest, and I'll bet when you come back you'll be excited about the job."

Lori frowned. If she said yes, would she be obligated to take a job that she wasn't sure she wanted? On the other hand, did she even *know* what she wanted? Maybe Clare was right, and the Cachet contract *was* too good to turn down. Maybe she *was* tired, and her priorities were a little confused just now. After all, she had come so far, so fast, and there had been so little opportunity to get used to the things that were happening to her. Maybe she just needed some time to think about it all—far away from cameras and costume designers and makeup people. And anyway, Clare might think she was ungrateful if she said no.

"Well," she said hesitantly, "I suppose I could. . . ."

"Wonderful!" Clare exclaimed, standing up. Her voice warmed. "I know you'll have a wonderful time, Lori. Being on Maui is like being in paradise. And when you come back, I promise that you'll have a whole new outlook. Believe me."

Lori returned Clare's smile uncertainly. "I'll try," she said.

Chapter Two

Lori got off the subway and made her way up the stairs and onto the busy street. It was nearly dark. The sleet had stopped, but the wind whipping around the buildings was icy cold. The fourth-floor apartment that Lori shared with Kit McCoy was only three blocks from the subway, and Lori usually loved the walk past small shops and exotic boutiques.

There was a flower shop on the corner that she especially liked. Back in Glenwood, where the plants grew green and fragrant all year, gardening had been one of Lori's favorite hobbies. Tonight her eye was caught by a tall, bright red flower, its bloom so brilliant and shiny it almost looked artificial. It was sitting in the steam-fogged window, wearing a sign that said: I'M AN ANTHERIUM, JUST IN FROM HAWAII.

Lori smiled. On the street around her, people were huddled in their winter coats, bending their heads into the wind, their noses and ears red from the cold. This flower had bloomed where the sun shone brightly all day long on white beaches lined with palm trees. A wave of excitement washed through her as she thought about her vacation. In just a few weeks, *she* would be in the islands, warmed by the sun and cooled by the breeze, enjoying a wonderful holiday in Clare Karlysle's condominium. In contrast to the dull, gray, chilly evening around her, the vision of a sunny beach seemed almost too good to be true. She needed something to remind her that it was actually going to happen. On an impulse, she went into the shop and bought the red antherium. When she came out again, carrying the flower wrapped in green paper, it was beginning to snow.

The two-bedroom apartment that Lori and Kit shared was small ("About the size of a doll's shoe box," Kit had joked when they moved in), but it was well laid out and attractive, with a tiny kitchen opening out onto a small rooftop patio that Lori had filled with plants during the summer. Now, the plants crowded the windows and every available shelf.

Lori hung her coat in the closet and went into the kitchen. Kit was already there, bending over the stove.

"M-m-m," Lori said, sniffing the spicy fragrance that came from the oven. "Smells super. What is it?"

Kit closed the oven door. "Oh, just lasagna," she said carelessly, grinning. "I'm trying a new recipe with feta cheese."

"Feta cheese," Lori said with a suspicious frown. "Isn't that *goat* cheese?"

"Now, now, Lori," Kit said, brushing a wisp of butterscotch-blond hair out of her eyes. "We're supposed to be living the grand adventure here in Greenwich Village, aren't we? Where's your adventurous spirit?"

Kit hadn't changed a bit since moving to New York City. She was enrolled in the dance program at the Juilliard School, and she was still the same colorful, outrageously-stylish Kit that she had always been. Her hair was tousled untidily in what Elaine used to call her Goldie Hawn look, and she was wearing a baggy red sweater over a blue turtleneck top, with black stirrup pants and ballet flats. Still, Kit's outsize clothes couldn't conceal her shapely figure. She couldn't understand how Kit could be so unconscious of calories. Kit never had to bother about her weight. Lori, on the other hand, had been on a constant diet for the last four years.

"I'm adventurous enough," she muttered,

"without going overboard on *goat* cheese."

"Oh, come on," Kit coaxed, taking down two stoneware plates from the cupboard. "You'll love it. In fact, you probably won't even notice the cheese, once you taste the spinach and pine nuts."

"Spinach? Nuts?" Lori exclaimed, horrified. "In lasagna?"

Kit shrugged. "I was getting tired of tomato sauce and meat. I thought it was time to break with tradition. And anyway, this lasagna has fewer calories."

Lori put down her green florist's bundle. "Any mail?" she asked, looking into the basket where the mail was kept.

"A two-page letter from Justin," Kit said, going to the refrigerator.

"So what else is new?" Lori asked with a playful smile. She leaned against the counter. Kit got a letter from Justin almost every day.

Justin was Kit's Glenwood High sweetheart. He was working in a biology lab in Palo Alto and studying pre-med at San Francisco State. They had been serious for the last year or so, and it looked to Lori as if they were going to stay that way, even though they were an entire continent apart. Lori sighed. Sometimes she wished for somebody who would care for her as much as Justin did for Kit. She could hardly imagine being so committed.

Just the week before, Kit had turned down an invitation from a good-looking neighbor to go ice-skating at Rockefeller Center because she wanted to be true to Justin.

Kit reached into the refrigerator and pulled out a plastic bag of salad greens and a couple of tomatoes. "What's that?" she asked, looking curiously at the green-wrapped flower lying on the counter. "Some new and exotic vegetable for our salad?"

"No," Lori said. "It's an antherium."

"A what?"

"An antherium, from Hawaii." She rummaged in the cupboard and found a pretty bowl and a needle holder. "I saw it in the window of the flower shop, and I couldn't resist."

Lori wanted to tell Kit her wonderful news, but she wasn't quite sure how to go about it. The two of them hadn't made any plans for Christmas, but she was certain that Kit was counting on the two of them spending the holidays together. Kit's job as a waitress in that little Italian restaurant down the street didn't leave her enough for a plane ticket back to Glenwood so she could be with Justin for Christmas. Kit was bound to be disappointed that her roommate wouldn't be in New York for the holidays.

Kit pulled the green paper off the flower. "Oh, wow. It's gorgeous." She handed it to

Lori, who trimmed the stem and placed it carefully on the needle holder in the bowl. "It makes me think of the tropics," Kit said wistfully. "Palm trees, sparkling water, and stuff like that."

It was all Lori could do to keep from spilling out her news, but she bit her tongue. "Yes, it does, doesn't it," she said, stepping back to look at the flower.

"Hey, Lori," Kit went on, walking to the sink to wash the salad greens, "Justin mentioned in his letter that one of the guys at work had a Hawaiian party, complete with a roast pig. Wouldn't that be fun for us to try? I could invite some of the kids from my classes at Juilliard, and you could ask some of the people you work with—models and photographers. We could have a *real* party."

Lori looked around the tiny kitchen. "Kit," she pointed out patiently, "there's hardly room for the two of us in this apartment. If each of us invited two people, somebody would have to stand out in the hall." She put the flower in the middle of the kitchen table. "Anyway, where would we roast the pig? Out on the roof on our hibachi?"

Kit made a face. "I guess it wasn't a very practical idea," she admitted, tearing a handful of red lettuce into a wooden bowl. "But to tell the truth, I'm beginning to feel a little penned up. I need a party, or something, especially with Christmas coming up." She glanced up at Lori. "You go out all the time. You probably don't know what I'm talking about."

"You go out sometimes," Lori reminded her, "to museums and shows and the ballet. And you could go out more if you'd say yes to some of the guys who ask you."

"Yeah, I know," Kit replied, with a sigh. She cut up a tomato into the salad. "But I can't. It wouldn't be fair to Justin."

"How do you know that Justin's not going out?"

Kit was unruffled by the question. "Because that's what we agreed," she said, putting the salad on the table. She opened the oven and took out the lasagna. "We agreed that we wouldn't go out with anybody else, at least for right now. Anyway, maybe it isn't that I want to go out. Maybe I just miss having lots of friends around. Maybe I just miss our old friends, like Elaine and Alex and Stephanie."

Lori pulled out a chair and sat down as Kit put the lasagna on the table. "I know what you mean," she said. "I was thinking of them today. I wonder what they're doing right now."

Kit sat down on the other side of the table

and began to dish out the lasagna. Lori eyed her plate suspiciously and took a tentative bite. She was surprised to find she liked its tangy flavor.

"Hey, Lori, I've been wondering where we're going to put our Christmas tree. There isn't much room. Unless we want to get rid of the sofa, it's going to have to be a *tiny* one." She wrinkled up her nose and handed the salad bowl to Lori. "About the size of a Dixie cup, maybe."

Lori laughed lamely, thinking about her vacation. She had to tell Kit, before Kit made any more plans for the holiday. "Kit, I'm afraid there's something I. . . ."

"Or maybe we could hang it from the ceiling," Kit said, with a burst of enthusiasm. "I'm serious. Today when I was coming home from class I saw a shop window that had a tree suspended from the. . ."

Lori put down the salad bowl. "There's something I have to tell you, Kit."

Kit looked downcast. "You don't like the lasagna," she said. "It's the goat cheese."

"No, it's not that at all. I—"

"Oh, wonderful!" Kit said, her blue eyes brightening. "I *knew* you would like it."

Lori closed her eyes briefly. "Yes, Kit, I *do* like the lasagna. But that's not what I'm trying to tell you, either."

"Oh. Then, what is it?"

Lori swallowed, feeling apprehensive. She began to wish that she hadn't agreed to Clare Karlysle's suggestion. Telling Kit was harder than she thought it was going to be. "The truth is," she said reluctantly, "I'm not going to be in New York for Christmas."

There was a long silence. "Not going to be in New York for Christmas?" Kit repeated finally, looking forlorn. "Where are you going? Do you have a shooting assignment over the holidays?"

Lori shook her head. "No," she said. This was *much* worse than she had thought. She stared at the red antherium in the middle of the table. "Actually, I've decided to take a little vacation. Clare Karlysle has offered to let me use her condo for the holidays. It . . . it's in Hawaii."

"Wow! Hawaii! So *that's* why you brought the flower home." Kit shook her head enviously. "Lori Woodhouse, your life is just one long lucky break! Gosh, I wish I could go with you."

"Well, I . . ."

Kit shook her head. "But it's out of the question," she sighed. "I could never afford anything like that." She grinned. "But I'm glad *one* of us can go, anyway. You'll have to take lots of pictures. And maybe you can

23

bring me a grass skirt or some shells or something so I'll feel as if I've been there with you. And you've got to promise that you'll send me a postcard every day to tell me what you're doing."

Feeling a sudden, sharp twinge of guilt, Lori looked at Kit. Even though she worked twice as many hours at the restaurant, Kit didn't make half as much money as Lori made for her modeling work. No matter how Kit saved and scrimped, she could never afford to go jetting off to Hawaii to stay in some luxurious condominium for a week. The kind of vacation that Lori was looking forward to was completely out of Kit's reach.

Or was it? With mounting excitement, Lori stared across the table at her roommate while Kit continued to talk. Why not treat Kit to a vacation as a Christmas present! Clare wouldn't mind; in fact, she would probably be delighted for Lori to have company. And with all the money Lori had saved, the extra plane ticket wouldn't be a problem. She leaned forward to interrupt Kit, the invitation on the tip of her tongue.

But then Lori hesitated. What if Kit felt overwhelmed by such a large gift? She was so generous that she would give the shirt off her back to help a friend, but she could never afford to give Lori anything nearly as expensive in return. The offer might embarrass her.

". . . Really, it's wonderful," Kit was saying. "And just wait until Alex and Elaine and Stephanie hear about this. They'll be so envious. . . ."

At the mention of their names, Lori suddenly knew what she would do. She would treat all *four* of her friends to a vacation in Hawaii, not just Kit. It had been months since they had seen one another, and this would be a *perfect* way for all of them to get together. A whole week in Hawaii, with her very best friends! With all the good modeling jobs she'd had lately, even three more plane tickets wouldn't be hard to manage.

". . . We'll put up the tree before you leave," Kit was going on. "And we could exchange our presents then. That way, we could at least have part of the holiday. . . ."

"I have a better idea," Lori interrupted, struggling to contain her excitement.

"A better idea? You think maybe we should wait until after you get back to open the presents?"

"Let's *all* go to Hawaii!"

Kit stared at Lori, her eyes growing large and round. "All *who*?"

"All of us! You and me, and Alex and Elaine and Stephanie. All five of us!"

Kit shook her head firmly. "It's a terrific

idea, Lori. But even if the condo is free, I can't afford the plane ticket, and I don't think the others can, either."

"But *I* can!" Lori jumped up, ran around the table, and threw her arms around Kit's neck. "I can, and I *want* to! It will be my Christmas present to everybody! The best Christmas we've ever had!"

Kit turned around in her chair. "Oh, Lori, it *would* be wonderful to spend the holidays together," she said, "but can you really afford it? I mean, it's a terrific expense."

Lori waved her hand. "Have you forgotten about those last two modeling jobs? Sure, I can afford it."

"But do you think everybody can go? I mean, what if the others have plans?"

"Well, let's find out," Lori said practically. She picked up the phone off the counter and brought it to the table. "We'll call Alex first, since she's only an hour behind us." She looked at the clock. "It's seven o'clock here, so it's six in Chicago. She ought to be home from diving practice by now."

Kit jumped up. "I'll get on the extension in the bedroom," she said. She looked down at Lori's plate. "Lori, you haven't finished your lasagna."

Lori picked up her fork with a rueful grin. "I guess Alex won't mind if I talk with my mouth full," she said.

The two girls spent most of the evening on the phone. Alex Enomoto, now at Northwestern University, where she was a member of the diving team, said yes immediately. Like Kit and Lori, she was delighted at the thought of escaping the northern winter for a few days. Alex's foster-sister, Stephanie, had to say no, because she'd already made other plans. But Elaine had agreed, too. She was almost through her first term at Stanford, and final exams would be over well before Christmas so she could definitely take a vacation. After consulting all of their parents, who of course were sorry that there wouldn't be any Christmas visits, everyone agreed that this trip was a once in-a-lifetime opportunity that shouldn't be passed up.

Finally, close to midnight, all the arrangements had been made. Tomorrow, Lori would tell Clare Karlysle that she wouldn't be making the trip alone. She would also call the travel agency and get tickets for everyone.

"Oh, Lori, I'm so happy," Kit said, as they brushed their teeth together in the bathroom, bumping elbows over the tiny sink. She stared into the mirror. "Christmas in Hawaii! I feel like I'm dreaming. It really sounds too good to be true."

"I know," Lori said. "Together again for Christmas. Won't it be terrific?" She glanced at her watch. "Oh, no, it's nearly midnight," she groaned. "I've got a seven-thirty shoot tomorrow, and I'll have horrible bags under my eyes."

"What are you shooting?" Kit asked, getting ready to wash her face.

Lori squeezed between Kit and the bathtub. "A suntan lotion ad," she said with a giggle. "On a fake sand beach in a third-floor photography studio on Forty-second Street, under fake palm trees and fake sunlight."

"That should only whet your appetite for the real thing," Kit said, bending over to scrub her forehead. "A real beach under the real sun."

"Sun," Lori repeated. She opened the blind and peered outside. In the circle of the streetlight, she could see the snow falling quietly on the deserted street. Already the cars and sidewalks were blanketed with it.

Chapter Three

"Would you like some coffee?"

Alex Enomoto looked up. "Uh, yes, please," she said, holding up her empty cup. When the willowy-looking stewardess had gone away with her lunch tray, she leaned back in her seat and looked out the airplane window, sipping the hot coffee gingerly from a Styrofoam cup. Outside the window, at 32,000 feet, the sky was full of dense white clouds. According to the pilot's announcement a few moments ago, they were flying over the Rockies, and the air was slightly turbulent.

Alex leaned forward, pushing her shoulder-length mahogany-colored hair back over her shoulder. She peered through the clouds, but she couldn't see even a trace of the steep mountains far below. It was snowing down there, she was sure, and cold. It was probably even colder than it had been when she'd left Chicago in the middle of a blizzard. Alex shivered. It had seemed to her like a blizzard, even though the local people said it was just snow flurries. In fact, she had almost missed her plane because the bus had gotten tied up in snow-clogged traffic a few blocks from O'Hare Airport. She had run as fast as she could to the gate, and even then, she was one of the last to board the big L-1011 that was taking her to Honolulu to meet her friends. She hoped that her luggage was making the same trip she was.

Alex sat back and put the half-empty coffee cup on the tray in front of her. She could hardly believe she was on her way to Hawaii for a vacation. She had been working extremely hard preparing for the Olympic trials, and even her college diving coach, demanding as he was, had had to admit that she deserved some time off for the holidays. Of all the members of the Northwestern women's diving team, Alex had racked up more hours in the pool than anyone.

Of course, she had a reason for working hard — *several* reasons, in fact. The most obvious one was her burning desire to make the Olympic trials next spring, and then after that, the Olympic team itself. Ever since she could remember, Alex had loved diving. In fact, she had been so involved with it for so long that she couldn't imagine a life without

steady himself. "I didn't notice that you were reading," he said, in an offended tone. "I'm sorry to have interrupted you." With a look that let her know he knew she was inventing an excuse not to talk to him, he went on down the aisle.

Alex shut the book. It wasn't that she had to study. There would be plenty of time for that later. It was just that she wasn't in the mood for any sort of personal encounter right then. You could never tell where they were going to lead, and she'd had enough of loving and losing. She didn't want any more close relationships in her life. They were too tough to handle when they fell apart. And her experience had taught her that that was exactly what happened. Every time. First there'd been Noodle, and then Danny and then . . .

"Our in-flight movie is about to begin," the stewardess announced over the PA system. "Tune into Channel 6 for the sound, and if you're next to a window, please pull down the shade. Thank you."

Alex put away her book and pulled down the shade, then turned her eyes on the big white screen at the front of the cabin. She was glad the movie was starting. She didn't want to follow her thoughts in the endless circle they always seemed to move in these days. She just wanted to relax and bury herself in some mindless entertainment. She settled back in her seat, adjusting her headset to Channel 6.

The movie opened with a close-up action shot of an auto racing crew in the pit, fueling a stock car as the driver pulled on his helmet and gave the thumbs-up sign. Alex winced and shifted uncomfortably in her seat. Race-tracks were part of what she wanted to forget—a big part. Tension mounting inside her, she watched the screen as the stock cars circled the track at enormous speeds, their roar nearly deafening in her ears. And then there was the inevitable horror, a car hurtling out of control, careening at full speed off a concrete wall, catapulting end-over-end in a shower of flying metal, and finally bursting into searing flame while ambulances raced toward the scene.

Alex shut her eyes against the image on the screen and wrenched the headset off. She squeezed back the tears forming under her eyelids. Seeing the crash on the screen brought everything back, like a tormenting nightmare she couldn't escape from, a frightening, recurring nightmare, of Wes Thorsen's horrible death and the agony that had haunted every minute of Alex's life since she had learned of it.

She had heard about Wes's accident in a

letter from Stephanie, two months ago. Wes had been burned to death when the race car he was driving had spun off the track and crashed into a fence. The car had been immediately engulfed in a fire so raging that the fire trucks were powerless against it. And the awful, unbearable irony was that Wes hadn't even been racing. He'd given it up because he had decided it was too dangerous, because he knew how much it frightened Alex. He had been testing a new engine when a tire blew. And now he was dead. The scene in the movie had brought it all painfully back to Alex.

She sat back in her seat, her eyes shut, her hands clenched in her lap. It was all over for Wes, she thought, but not for *her.* The time that she and Wes had been in love had been both the happiest and the most miserable time of her life. She had been deliriously happy when they were together. Wes had been the only one in her life who understood her need to compete and win, for he was driven by the same need. She had been miserable and frightened when Wes was racing, or when they had fought about his racing.

Now that he was gone, she was determined never to feel such misery ever again—and the easiest way to be sure was to keep herself from getting close to anyone. First there had been the pain of her brother, Noodle's, death from cystic fibrosis. No matter how hard she tried, she knew she would never get over the feeling of desolation that had come over her when he had died. She remembered how she had felt that day. It was as if she had died, too, and the person who was walking around was a different Alex, an Alex who had to live without Noodle. Now she had to endure the pain of Wes's death, too. There was a price to be paid for loving someone, a very high price. Alex only knew that she didn't want to pay it anymore.

She sat up and pulled a tissue from her pocket to blow her nose, turning away from the movie screen and pushing the thought of the crash from her mind. This was exactly why she needed a vacation, she reminded herself. She had been training harder than ever since she had learned of Wes's death, trying to forget her misery in her diving. That could only work for a while, because she was physically wearing herself out. Now she was going to try something else for a change. She was going to *play* hard. She was going to enjoy this Christmas with Lori, Kit, and Elaine.

A smile crossed Alex's face. She'd missed them all so much. It seemed as if a lifetime had passed by since they'd stood together on the platform in the Glenwood gym at the end of their senior year, wearing their caps and gowns, receiving their diplomas with hugs and tears. She could hardly believe it when she had gotten the call from Lori a couple of weeks ago, inviting her to come to Hawaii for the Christmas holidays. It was exactly what she needed, although she'd never have been able to afford it herself. But it was just like Lori to be thoughtful and generous and share the good things that were happening to her now that her modeling career was going so well.

Alex reached into her bag and pulled out the letter from her foster-sister, Stephanie. Stephanie was still back at Glenwood, making what she laughingly called a "second run" at her senior year. She had moved from one foster family to another before she came to live with the Enomotos, and her transcript looked like a crazy quilt. She had decided that it would be easier to get into a good college if she got another solid year of high school behind her. Even though she was unable to join her friends in Hawaii, it sounded as though she wouldn't be suffering too much.

Alex opened the letter and began to read. She could almost hear Stephanie's lively voice coming through and see her brown eyes dancing with excitement.

Dear Alex,

Wow! A trip to Hawaii to stay in some posh beachfront condo with Lori and Kit and Elaine!! Sounds almost too good to be true!!! And I'm afraid it is (sigh), at least for me. You'll just have to soak up my quota of fun (and sunburn — you know how I freckle) and track my share of sand into the house. (Boy, how about that Lori, picking up all those incredible modeling jobs? Pretty soon we're going to be seeing her face on billboards. Wouldn't you love to spend a week in New York with her and Kit and see what their lives are like?)

As for me, I'll be spending the holidays with Rick at the Forresters' Bear Valley lodge. Isn't that a kick? I'm really excited about it!! But of course, I'm a nervous wreck, too. I am an absolute and total klutz on skis, and even the idea of standing at the top of a slope and looking down gives me vertigo. (I've never understood how you could get up on the ten-meter board.) But Rick claims he's an expert and he promises to teach me everything he knows. (Everything he knows about how to crash, probably!) Anyway, I firmly expect to break a leg on my very first downhill run, so that I won't have to make the second. I'll save room on my cast for your signature.

In the meantime, I hereby command you to have the time of your life in Hawaii. I understand that every outdoor sport known to man (and woman!) is played there— tennis, volleyball, surfing—and some wonderful indoor sports, too, which I guess I don't need to mention here (ha ha). I hope that you'll indulge, and get your mind off everything that's happened lately. I have this very definite feeling that you've been drowning yourself in your work (so to speak) and that all your thoughts are very serious ones. You are forbidden to have any serious thoughts in Hawaii. You're to go surfing every day, and not think.

And speaking of surfing, that's where all the action is in Hawaii, according to my informants. It's also where all the best-looking boys are. So for the best boy-hunting in Hawaii, all you have to do is find out where the surf is running and hang out there!!!

Lots of love,
* Steph*

Alex folded up the letter with a wistful smile. Well, if she couldn't see Steph this Christmas, she would see her next May, at Glenwood's commencement. *That* was something she had promised herself not to miss, regardless of her training schedule. Right now, she had every intention of following Stephanie's instructions to the letter — except for one thing. She was going to cross boy-hunting off her list. As a sport, it was definitely too dangerous.

Chapter Four

Elaine Gregory perched on the edge of her seat in the boarding lounge at San Francisco International Airport waiting for her flight to Honolulu to be called. She was surrounded by a small army of friends. Red-haired, bouncy Ginger Goodman was there, along with several current Glenwood High students: Rayne Ramirez, Lani Connors, Nancy Colton, and Gloria Larsen, who had volunteered her battered yellow-and-green VW bus for the trip to the airport.

Elaine had become friends with this year's crop of seniors when she had served as the counselor for the Seniors' Orientation Weekend at Rainbow Lake. Now that Elaine was studying at Stanford University, she didn't see them very often, except for Rayne, whom she was tutoring. She was anxious to catch up with what was going on in their lives.

"Ta-ta-ta-tatata," Ginger trumpeted, as the

excited girls clustered around Elaine. "Okay, gather 'round, gang, it's time for the presentations!"

"Presentations? What presentations?"

"You didn't think you'd get away without a Glenwood-style going-away party, did you?" Rayne asked, tossing her dark hair. Rayne was a real Latin beauty who never behaved as if she knew she was beautiful.

"We want you to be *sure* to have the best vacation in the whole world," Lani Connors said, stepping forward importantly. "So we're here to help." She turned to Ginger. "Okay, Ginger, you're on."

Ginger held up a brightly decorated tin. "For a tasty Hawaiian holiday," she said, handing the tin to Elaine with an elegant flourish.

"What is it?" Elaine asked, opening the lid and sniffing.

"It's a new recipe that I concocted especially for this occasion," Ginger replied. Ginger ran her own successful gourmet cookie business in Glenwood and was constantly forcing batches of her famous recipes on her friends. "Macadamia nut macaroons. There's enough there for everybody — well, for three people, anyway. I know that Lori won't touch any for fear of getting fat so Lani's brought something especially for Lori."

Curiously, Elaine turned over the little tin-foil package that Lani handed her. "What's this?"

"Celery and carrot sticks," Lani said, barely containing her laughter. "Lifted from the Glenwood cafeteria. We thought that Lori might want something to remind her of home—especially since she won't eat the macaroons."

"Okay, who's next," Ginger asked.

"Me," Rayne announced, as she pulled a red-and-pink paper lei from her bag. "It might be a little crushed," she said cheerfully, draping it around Elaine's neck, "since I've been carrying it around for a few days. But it's the spirit that counts."

"Gee, thanks, Rayne," Elaine muttered, feeling a little conspicuous with the scratchy crepe paper around her neck.

"I've brought you something else," Rayne said, rummaging in her bag. "Now, what did I *do* with it?" After a minute she pulled out a paper. "Here it is," she said triumphantly. "My trig test! I got a ninety-eight—the top grade in the class. And it's all thanks to you, Elaine!"

"That's terrific, Rayne!" Elaine hugged her, feeling a sharp surge of pride. "But give yourself some credit. You're the one who pulled this off. Congratulations!"

"Thanks." Rayne folded her paper and put it back in her bag.

"Hey, Elaine." Nancy spoke up. "I've been meaning to ask your advice about something. I'm thinking of starting a Personals column in the *Call*. You know, where kids could advertise." Nancy was the editor of the school newspaper, *The Glenwood Call*.

"Advertise what?" Lani asked curiously.

Nancy blushed. "Oh, you know," she said. "Advertise . . . advertise for . . . for friendship and dates and stuff like that."

"Oh, you mean a *sex* column!" Lani exclaimed. "Like the one in the Glenwood newspaper." She put a finger to her chin, thinking out loud. " 'Lonely junior male desires lonely junior female for after-school partying. Must have weird sense of humor and adore Dungeons and Dragons.' Something like that?"

"Well, not quite like that, but that's the idea," Nancy said. "The column would be a place where kids could . . ."

"Could advertise for a boyfriend or girlfriend?" Lani suggested.

Nancy shook her head. "I give up," she said, rolling her eyes. She appealed to Elaine. "What do *you* think of the idea, Elaine?"

Elaine shrugged. "I don't know," she replied uncertainly. "I guess, if everybody understood the ground rules . . ." Before Elaine could finish her sentence, a mechanical-sounding voice came over the loudspeakers:

"Flight 409 for Honolulu is now boarding. Please have your passes ready for the attendant at the gate."

"That's me." Elaine stood up and slung her carry-on luggage over her shoulder.

"Have a wonderful time!" Rayne said, with a hug.

"Send postcards," Lani admonished.

"Give everybody my love," Ginger shouted, as Elaine started down the ramp. "If they like the macaroons, maybe we could talk about setting up a franchise in New York or Chicago!"

Elaine's seat was at the front of the plane, and she settled into it with a contented sigh, fingering the paper lei that Rayne had placed around her neck. She had such wonderful friends—and not only the group that had come to see her off, but the three that she was going to see when the plane landed in Honolulu! Lori, Kit, and Alex, her very *best* friends, the friends she had shared so much with over the years.

How many years? She thought back. She and Kit and Alex had been together since sixth grade, when Alex had christened them the Three Nutsketeers. Then when Lori had come along in their junior year, they had called themselves the Fearless Four. They'd been inseparable—until graduation had pulled them apart. And now Lori was helping them get back together again.

Lori. A warm feeling flooded through Elaine as she thought about Lori. To think that Lori's modeling career was so successful that she could afford to treat her friends to a spectacular trip like this one. This vacation was the most fantastic present that anyone had ever given Elaine. It was even better than Munchkin, the kitten that her first boyfriend, Carl, had given to her, or the gold necklace Zack had put around her neck just before he moved to L.A. to make movies.

Elaine fingered the necklace she was wearing under her tailored red blouse. She and Zack had spent a wonderful summer in Arizona, where he had filmed a low-budget Western and she had helped him spot locations. When they got back, Zack had been offered a job at a well-known Hollywood studio with a group of filmmakers he really respected.

"I don't want to leave you," Zack had said when he gave her the news. His fingers had tightened on her arm. "But it's an opportunity I can't pass up."

"I know," Elaine had said. "And you

shouldn't. It's a chance for you to show every-body how good you are. But we can write. And of course there's always the telephone."

"Yeah," Zack said, after pausing for a moment. "But I think . . . I mean, it would be better if we weren't quite so . . . I mean, if we . . ." His voice had trailed off, and he looked red-faced and uncomfortable.

"If we dated other people?" Elaine had asked.

Zack had looked at her in grateful surprise. "Yeah, that's what I was trying to say. How did you know?"

"Because I think that's what we ought to do, too," Elaine had answered, glad that he felt the same way she did. She had thought that he might be angry. "I was trying to figure out how to say it to you."

It wasn't that she didn't love Zack, she had told herself, on the drive back down the Peninsula. She had even begun to wonder if she didn't love him too much. The summer had been a magical one, and they had been so close.

After they got home, Elaine had decided her life was becoming much too narrow. She'd hardly had a chance to see the world, and here she was, getting really serious about one guy. So she'd actually been glad when Zack had told her about the tremendous offer in L.A. It had taken some of the pressure off, and she'd begun to look forward to dating more than one guy at a time—quite a switch for Elaine Gregory.

Since Zack left, Elaine had been getting letters from him about his exciting life in Hollywood. In comparison, her own life seemed like one constant, dull grind of work and study. She had a work-study scholarship to Stanford, and under its terms she had to work twenty hours a week in the library. Between putting books on the shelves for other people to study and studying books herself, Elaine had begun to feel like Marian the Librarian in *The Music Man*. She'd only been to one football game, and the season was already over! And because she lived at home with her family and commuted, she hadn't made nearly as many friends as she wanted to. As far as dating more than one guy was concerned, forget it. She hadn't even had time to date *one*!

In fact, living at home with her sisters Andrea, Chrissie, and Carla made her college life seem very much like her high school life, except that classes were harder and teachers' expectations higher. And she'd been so busy that she hadn't had time to pay much attention to her appearance. She'd even gone back to wearing her old preppie-drab clothes, because when she left for the library early in the morning it was easier to reach into the closet for whatever was handy than to create something imaginative out of what she found hanging there. But before she went completely back to her old ways, she had decided to put a stop to it, become more stylish, and last week she'd gone on a shopping trip for new clothes. She'd even bought a new pair of contact lenses. She had started wearing contacts last year, but she'd lost one down the drain, and for the past three months she hadn't even bothered to replace them.

Next to Zack's life filled with pool parties, beach parties, cast parties and trips to Acapulco and Mazatlan, Elaine's life had become positively monastic. She felt an unmistakable stab of jealousy every time she read one of his letters. She had images of him surrounded by half-a-dozen young starlets at poolside.

Well, if she wasn't leading an exciting life, it was her own fault, Elaine thought, pulling a flight magazine out of the seat pocket in front of her. The trouble was that casual dating had never been her style. Unlike some of the girls she knew—Cheryl Abrahamson, for instance—she'd never been able to play the field and enjoy whatever came along. As a result, she'd only had two boyfriends in her life, Carl and Zack, and both of those relationships had been very intense and very serious. She'd had a brief fling once, when she and Carl had decided to date other people, but it had been a disaster and she hadn't been eager to try it again.

But now she thought she might finally be ready. Couldn't she just fool around without falling in love? There wasn't anything wrong with having a quick, short-term romance. Other people did it.

For a moment, Elaine pushed aside her usual cautious self and let herself fantasize about meeting someone...someone with whom she could have the perfect fling—a just-for-fun, no-strings-attached romantic adventure. It could happen in Hawaii, she told herself. In fact, now that she thought about it, Hawaii was exactly the kind of romantic setting where it *ought* to happen!

At that moment, the attractive man sitting across the aisle from her looked over and smiled, his eyes warm. "On your way to the islands?" he asked, with a quick glance at the lei around her neck.

Elaine smiled back, a strange, giddy sense of freedom sweeping over her. She felt different, somehow. She felt *ready*. Ready for life, ready for love. Ready to see what the world was all about. "Yes," she said, relaxing. "And I'm really looking forward to it."

Chapter Five

The plane dipped low across Mamala Bay as it prepared to touch down on the long offshore runway at Honolulu International Airport.

"Look! It's Diamond Head!" Kit said excitedly, peering out the plane window. The extinct volcano loomed up over seven hundred feet above the ocean, guarding the southern tip of Oahu, the island on which the city of Honolulu was located. "And there's Waikiki Beach," she said, pointing. "Look at how *white* the sand is."

Lori leaned forward, looking out the window over Kit's shoulder. "It looks as if there're more sunbathers than sand down there," she said. "I'm glad we're going to Maui. Clare says it's a lot less crowded than Oahu, and that the beaches are even better than Waikiki. Much more private."

As the plane landed, Kit ran a comb

through her unruly hair, wishing she'd taken the time to brush it in front of the mirror in the tiny rest room. She got out her compact and tried to repair the damage she had done to her mascara when she rubbed her eyes. The trip had taken nearly ten hours, and they had crossed a whole bunch of different time zones. She had been napping for a while but her weariness disappeared as the plane taxied up to the jetway.

"I still can't believe it," Kit said, hiking her bag up over her shoulder. "It just seems too good to be true." In fact, she thought, as she and Lori moved out of their seats and into the crowded aisle, her whole *life* these days seemed like a glorious dream: her work at Juilliard, the cute little apartment in the Village, her relationship with Justin. She glanced into her bag.

Justin's last letter was still there, already beginning to look worn and dingy from being read so many times. She had nearly told Lori her startling news a dozen times on the long plane trip, but she had managed to keep it to herself. She wanted to tell everybody at once and get her friends' advice about what she ought to do. What Justin was saying *sounded* so right, but she just wasn't sure. Something her mother had told her once flashed through her mind: "When in doubt, don't."

She pushed the thought aside. She might not be ready to say yes, but she wasn't ready to say no, either.

"Do you suppose they'll be waiting for us here, or in the main terminal?" Lori asked from behind Kit, interrupting her thoughts.

"It depends on what time they got in," Kit said, over her shoulder. The passengers began to make their way out of the plane and up the long ramp. At the end of the jetway, the door opened onto a large, glassed-in waiting area filled with huge green plants that made the terminal look like a tropical rain forest.

"There they are!" Lori said excitedly, pointing into the crowd. "I see them! They're already here! They're waiting for us!"

"Alex! Elaine!" Kit screamed, jumping up and down. With a frantic rush, she ran toward her friends and threw her arms around both of them. "Oh, I can't believe it! I can't believe it!" she cried jubilantly. She did a delighted little dance. "It's too good to be true!"

"Lori, what a wonderful Christmas present!" Alex exclaimed, giving Lori a hug. "I've felt like I've been in *exile* up there in the freezing Midwest, away from all of you." She waved her arms gleefully, looking around her. "Look at all these people—most of them look just like me!"

Kit glanced around. It was true—well over

53

half of the crowd milling around them had Oriental features and the delicately golden skin of Polynesian and Oriental peoples.

"They even have a special name for white people here," Elaine said, holding up a guide-book. "They call us *haoles*. It means something like 'paleface.'" Lori, Kit, and Alex exchanged glances. It was just like bookish Elaine to be feeding them information already. She even looked like a tour guide, with her long-sleeved red blouse and sensible tailored skirt, her dark brown hair pinned back with the familiar tortoiseshell clip. And she had gone back to her tortoiseshell glasses again. She must have given up her contacts. Kit shook her head in amazement.

"Elaine, you haven't changed a bit," she said.

"Oh, yes, I have," Elaine retorted. "I mean, at least I *will*. You just wait and see." With that mysterious remark, she gave Kit a long, assessing look. "You haven't changed, either," she said with a grin. "You look exactly like the same sexy Kit. Pity the poor, help-less boys out there on the beaches. They don't know what they've got in store for them!"

Kit looked down at her clothes. She was wearing a pair of tight designer jeans and a clingy yellow T-shirt over a pink tank top. "Thanks . . . I think," she said. She never thought of herself as sexy, and was always taken by surprise when a boy whistled at her or gave her a suggestive look.

Elaine gave Lori an ecstatic hug. "Ginger Goodman sends her love," she said. "I mean, her *aloha*. Actually," she added, glancing down at the guidebook, "her *aloha nui*. Lots of love and hugs and a huge tin of Macadamia macaroons!"

Lori shook her head. "That's great, but I don't think I . . ."

"It's okay, Lori," Elaine said, patting her on the shoulder. "Some of this year's seniors sent some celery and carrot sticks for you— straight from the Glenwood High cafeteria!"

"Oh, no," Kit moaned. "You've got to be kidding! Here we fly all the way from New York to Hawaii, only to find that a bunch of celery sticks from the good old Glenwood cafeteria have beaten us here? How ridiculous!"

"Listen, celery sticks are *not* such a bad idea," Lori said seriously. "With all the rich food they served us on the airplane, I'm beginning to feel like a . . ."

Alex eyed her friend's figure. "Lori, that's enough," she said firmly. "You look absolutely terrific. And a vacation is not for dieting." She laughed. "I can see that *you* haven't changed. Except that you look a little more . . ." She hesitated. "I mean, you sound . . ."

"More self-confident?" Lori suggested, with the trace of a smile.

Alex colored.

Kit threw back her head and laughed. "It's okay, Alex. You can take your foot out of your mouth now."

Alex managed a lame smile. "I'm sorry. I just meant. . . ."

"Don't apologize," Lori interrupted. "You're right. When I first came to New York, I felt like a little girl fresh out of some tiny town in the hills or something. I was completely lost, and I was sure I was going to be a big flop. But Clare really helped me out in the first few weeks. She made me feel a lot more confident in my own abilities. She even talked me into taking voice lessons, to cure the little-girl voice I've had all my life. And all of a sudden I realized I wasn't so scared anymore."

"Clare?" Elaine said. "Who's she?"

"Haven't I mentioned her in my letters?" Lori asked. "She's the woman who owns the condo where we'll be staying when we get to Oahu. She runs CHIC, the modeling agency I work for."

Kit looked around. The crowd was beginning to thin out a little. "Speaking of Oahu," she said, "how do we get there? Swim? Take a boat?"

"What's the matter, Kit? Didn't you read

your ticket?" Elaine teased.

Kit blushed. She knew she had a reputation for being scatterbrained and not always as together as the others. "I guess not," she confessed meekly.

"We fly," Elaine said. A smile hovered at the corners of her mouth. "But first we have to *holoholo* a *wikiwiki* bus to the main terminal, where we catch our plane."

Kit stared at her. "*Holoholo* a *wikiwiki* bus?" She turned to the others. "Is Elaine's tongue all tangled up, or do my ears have jet lag?"

"*Wikiwiki* is the Island word for hurry hurry," Elaine said. She held up the guidebook. "And *holoholo* means to ride. So we're going to ride on the hurry-hurry buses that take people to the main terminal for inter-island flights."

Kit glanced at her watch. "I don't know about the rest of you," she said, "but I don't want to miss a minute of this wonderful vacation. So I vote that we *wikiwiki*! On the double!"

The girls settled into their seats on the smaller turbo- prop Aloha Airlines plane that would take them to Maui. They had been lucky enough to find facing seats at the front of the plane, so they could carry on their conversation. They had been chattering nonstop ever since their planes landed, trying to catch up on one another's lives.

Kit was almost bursting with her own exciting news, and as soon as Elaine got back from a trip to the rest room she broke into the conversation.

"Listen, you guys," she said urgently, leaning toward Alex and Elaine, who were sitting across from her. "I've got something I want to discuss with you. Something *very* important."

Alex sipped a soft drink the stewardess had brought her. "Go ahead," she commanded. "We're all ears."

Kit pulled Justin's letter out of her bag. "Well," she said slowly, fingering it, "it's about Justin." She had been so impatient to tell them, but now that she had their attention, she was oddly nervous.

"Don't tell me that you two have broken up," Alex said regretfully.

"No," Kit said. "We're still together. More so, in fact, than ever before."

"That's *really* a long-distance love affair," Elaine said. "How do you manage it? I mean, are you seeing anyone else?"

"Are you kidding?" Lori asked. She shook her head, with an affectionate glance at Kit, who was sitting next to her. "Kit has become the original stay-at-home gal. She turns down a couple of dates a week in order to be faithful to Justin. And their postage bill is phenomenal. They're probably keeping the postal service afloat, just the two of them, with all the letters that go back and forth."

Kit sat up straighter and squared her shoulders. "You guys all know that Justin and I decided last summer before I went to New York that we wouldn't date anybody else. And . . . well, now he wants to make it official." She looked around to see their reaction. "He wants to be engaged."

"Engaged!" the others exclaimed in unison.

Anxiously, Kit glanced at each of their faces. They all looked surprised, and they weren't exactly jumping up and down with approval.

She put the letter away. She had planned to read the best part of it to them, but now she wasn't sure she wanted to. "Of course, it would have to be a pretty long engagement, until we're both through college." Kit wrinkled her nose. "After that, he's got medical school, and you know how long *that* takes. But he wants to, he says, because it will make us more sure of ourselves, and easier to say no to other people."

"Well, do you think it will?" Alex demanded, leaning forward in her seat.

"Do I think it will what?" Kit asked.

"Make it easier to say no to other people," Alex replied.

Kit shrugged. "I don't know. I guess so." She took a sip of her soft drink. "Although I don't seem to have all that much trouble saying no now."

"But maybe Justin does," Elaine put in.

Kit looked at her. "What do you mean?"

Elaine shifted uncomfortably. "Well, maybe Justin's finding it kind of hard not to date other people. Maybe he doesn't have as much willpower as you do and he thinks that the security of an engagement would help him."

"Help him fend off the other girls, you mean?" Kit asked, with a helpless giggle at the sudden, incongruous image of Justin Kennerly with a long pole, beating off a half dozen clamoring girls.

"Well, something like that," Elaine said.

"Or maybe he feels uncertain about *you*," Alex observed. "Maybe he wants to tie *you* down so you won't change your mind about him."

Lori looked at her. "How do *you* feel about getting engaged?" she asked. "Is it what you want to do?"

Kit shook her head uncertainly. She appreciated Lori's quiet way of getting right to the heart of things. "I don't know," she said slowly. "I mean, I really love Justin. There's no doubt in my mind about that. I've loved him for a long time. And there's no room for anyone else in my life right now, no matter how much distance there is between Justin and me." She paused, wanting to be completely honest with her friends, and with herself. "But I have the feeling that if I don't say yes, I might lose him. You know how Justin is about planning things and being logical and all that. When he makes up his mind to something, it's pretty hard to get him to budge. The letter sounds like he's given this engagement a lot of thought and it's something he *really* wants. If I say no, I'm not sure what he'll do."

"But on the other hand...?" Lori prompted.

Kit smiled, grateful for Lori's help. "But on the other hand, I guess I wonder whether we're ready for something as important as an engagement. Even if we *have* been practically engaged for the last year."

There. Now that it was all said, she could relax a little. She smiled and stretched. "This vacation is really going to be good for me," she said. "It'll give me a week to think about this before I decide."

"Only a week!" Alex asked, startled. "Is

that all the time you're going to take to think about this?"

Kit dropped her eyes. "Well, I told Justin I would give him my answer right after the holiday. I'm going to stop in Glenwood on the way back to New York and visit him and his folks." She sipped the last of her drink. "I ought to be able to decide something by then," she said.

"Well, maybe so," Alex conceded. "But I think you ought to take your time. I mean, being engaged is just a step away from being married. And *that's* pretty final."

"Final!" Elaine shuddered. "It's almost like being dead, if you ask me."

The other girls stared at her in amazement. "Dead?" Lori said. "Is this the same Elaine who was ecstatic about spending the entire summer with her boyfriend, Zack, out in the Arizona desert so they could get closer?"

"And the same Elaine who went with Carl for almost a year before she started going with Zack?" Kit asked. "The same Elaine who wrote her psychology paper for Mrs. Wiseman last year on the virtues of early marriage?"

Elaine regarded the others thoughtfully. "No," she said, definitively. "It is definitely *not* the same Elaine."

Alex leaned toward her friend. She'd been watching Elaine for the last few minutes, and she had the feeling that something about her had changed. "Elaine, aren't your eyes usually a different color?" she asked. "What happened to the *amber* eyes you've had for the last eighteen years? The eyes you've gone back to hiding behind those tortoiseshell glasses."

"My brown eyes are still there," Elaine explained. "You just can't see them. They're under the new green contacts I put in when I went to the rest room a minute ago."

"Green contacts!" Kit squealed, leaning close to see for herself. "This is as earthshaking a change as the time you got that beauty makeover!"

"What's going *on* with you, Elaine?" Lori asked. "Why did you decide to get green eyes?"

"Because I'm tired of amber eyes," Elaine exclaimed. "And I'm tired of brown skirts and brown sweaters and brown shoes. I'm tired of being Marian the Librarian for sixteen hours a day. And most of all, I'm tired of selling my soul to Stanford University, just so I can get a degree in four years." She stretched luxuriously, like a cat. "I've come to Hawaii to have some fun for a change! I'm looking for men! I want a *fling*! The wilder the better!"

"The wilder the better?" Kit repeated in consternation. "Wow, was I wrong when I said you hadn't changed."

"What does Marian the Librarian have to do with it?" Lori asked.

"While we were waiting for you, Elaine told me that she spends half her time shelving books and the other half *studying* them," Alex explained. "She's beginning to feel left out of things." She turned to Elaine. "Listen, I can understand how you feel. It's the same way for me at Northwestern. I spend half my day in the classroom and half of it in the pool. There's no time left for anything else."

"Exactly," Elaine said, with a grim edge to her voice. "And I'm beginning to *hate* it."

Alex shook her head. "I'm not. The more work the better. That's the way I like it. I didn't come to Hawaii to look for men. I'm through with romance. Absolutely finished. I'm just here to relax and get enough sun to last me until June." She grinned. "The sun apparently never shines on Chicago between the months of November and June. Maybe that's why there are so many *haoles* up there. By the time winter is over, everybody's a pale-face."

Elaine turned to Lori. "*I've* come to Hawaii to have a wild fling. Kit's come to try to decide whether to say yes or no to Justin. Alex has come to get a suntan. Why are you here?"

Lori looked out the window. "I have to decide whether or not to take a big modeling job," she said, "with Cachet Cosmetics. They're launching a new line, and they want to sign me to a long-term contract. Clare would like me to do it, because it would be good for my career and it would mean a big commission for the agency. When I said I didn't want to, she thought I was overworked and must need a vacation. So she offered me the use of her condo for the holidays."

Alex frowned. "So what's to decide?" she asked. "The contract sounds like a terrific opportunity to me."

"Yeah," Kit said, trying to read Lori's gaze. Lori hadn't said anything to her about this new contract, but she wasn't surprised. Lori was sometimes very private. "What's the problem? I thought you were anxious to get the big, important modeling jobs."

Lori spread her hands. "Well, I thought I was," she said, shaking her head. "But this modeling hasn't turned out quite the way I thought it would. I mean, I like it, but it isn't as rewarding as some other things I like to do, like painting."

"You want to become an artist?" Elaine asked.

"You want to give up a glamorous, high-paying job to become a poor, starving artist?" Alex amended.

"But you've wanted to be a model forever," Kit said. "Now that you've finally got what you want, are you sure you want to throw it all away?" She was truly puzzled. Even after living with Lori for five months, she hadn't detected the slightest trace of her unhappiness.

Lori gave them a weak smile. "No, I'm not sure," she said. "I don't even know whether I've got any talent or not." She patted her flight bag. "But I brought my sketch pad and some pencils. I thought that while I was here, I'd have a chance to draw. And think a little, too."

Alex looked out the plane window. "It sounds as if we have our assignments cut out for us," she said. "This is going to be an interesting vacation."

Chapter Six

The plane to Maui made the trip in less than a half hour, flying over miles of the bluest water that Lori had ever seen. Viewed from the air, the island looked like an oddly shaped emerald brooch, ringed with golden beaches and studded at either end with the dark masses of sleeping volcanoes.

"That crater over there is called Haleakala," Elaine said, reading from her guidebook. "The name means House of the Sun. It's the largest dormant volcano in the world. It says here that you could put all of Manhattan Island into the crater and the tallest skyscraper wouldn't rise over the rim."

"Let's hope it stays dormant," Lori said as the plane came down for a landing. "At least as long as we're here."

Elaine laughed. "Oh, I don't think we're in any danger," she said. "The last explosion was over two thousand years ago."

The Kahului airport was small, and the passengers stepped off the plane directly onto the field in the late afternoon sunlight. They were greeted by an energetic group of small boys selling white and purple orchid leis, and the girls bought several fragrant wreaths to drape around their necks. Their bags appeared on the luggage conveyer after a few minutes, and they carried them to the rental car desk. Lori had made arrangements for a car, a bright red compact hatchback that was parked in front of the airport. By the time all four of them stowed their bags in the back and climbed in, the car was packed full.

Lori looked around, trying to see the girls wedged into the back seat, under the bags, and couldn't help laughing. "It's the Fearless Four, together again," she said. "Maui, watch out!"

"This reminds me of the hundreds of times we squished ourselves into the Pokey Pumpkin," Alex said, trying to cram her flight bag between her feet in the back seat. The Pokey Pumpkin was Kit's little orange VW.

"I suppose somebody knows where we're going," Elaine remarked from the back seat.

"Oh, I have a rough idea," Lori replied, consulting the map that Clare Karlysle had given her before she left, along with the keys to the condo. "We're headed for Kaanapali Beach, on the west coast of the island. It's only about a half hour drive, and there's just one road going in that direction, so I don't think there's any danger of getting lost." She handed Kit the map. "Would you be our navigator?"

Route 30, which took them to Kaanapali, turned out to be a beautiful scenic highway, through the most gorgeous landscape that any of them had ever seen. For part of the way, the road wound along the sea, sometimes suspended a hundred feet above the ocean rocks, sometimes dipping down into the tropical jungle. The dense green foliage pressed in on both sides, with guava and monkeypod trees, fern, bamboo, banana plants, and papaya growing right up to the road. The bright blossoms of hibiscus and red-and-yellow plumerias spiked the green foliage with brilliant bursts of color. On the left, the surf pounded against rugged lava shores or lapped softly up the sloping sand beaches. After a while, they got tired of ooh-ing and aah-ing and rode in silence, looking wide-eyed out the windows.

"Looks like this is it," Kit said a little while later, pointing to a sloping driveway half-hidden by huge philodendra. They had stopped at a grocery store a few miles back, and the car, already packed full, was now additionally loaded with snacks and bottles of soft drinks and the makings of sandwiches and salads.

Lori pulled up in front of the condo, a two-story white-stucco building perched on a cliff overlooking the beach. It was surrounded by dense clusters of fern, and the trellis around it was covered with flowering vines. A huge banyon tree sheltered the brick patio, and a small fountain tinkled musically beside the carved wooden door. Lori unlocked the door, and they all trooped inside, loaded down with luggage.

"Oh, wow," Lori breathed. For a moment she just stood, speechless. The living room was a solid wall of windows, and beyond the windows the blue ocean stretched to the horizon, where the sun was setting in a towering billow of pink and gold cloud, delicate as a shell. The waves breaking on the reef that sheltered the beach were tinged by the sun's pink, and even the sand seemed to glow with a shell-like luminescence. The rest of the girls joined Lori at the window, and they stood for a few moments quietly, drinking in the beauty of the sea and the sky.

Kit was the first to break the silence. "*Wow* is right," she said, glancing around. "This place is incredible!" There was a wide-screen TV in one corner of the elegant living room, a rattan sofa and chairs upholstered in a bright floral print, and gold chrome and glass end and coffee tables. "Hey, look!" she said. "Flowers! Somebody has sent us a big bouquet of flowers!"

Lori turned away from the window. "They must be from Clare. But why would *she* send us flowers?"

The girls clustered around the coffee table to look at the huge, rainbow-hued bouquet of tropical blossoms, heavy with scent. "Here's a card," Alex said, picking up a little white envelope and handing it to Lori. "It's addressed to you."

Curiously, Lori opened the envelope and pulled out the card. "Welcome to Paradise," it said, in a strong, masculine hand. It was signed "Kevin Duvall."

"Kevin Duvall?" Kit said. She giggled. "Lori, you've been keeping secrets from us again, haven't you? Who is this guy?"

Lori blushed. "I don't have the slightest idea." She looked at the flowers spilling over the rim of the vase.

"Well, we know one thing," Elaine said. "Whoever Kevin Duvall is, he has remarkably good taste in flowers."

"And plenty of money," Alex added, bending down to sniff. "Flowers like this don't come cheap—even in Paradise."

"Well, I vote that we table this mystery for a while and go exploring out on the beach before it gets too dark," Kit suggested, picking up her shoulder bag. "I'm going to change." With a chorus of agreement, the others followed her eagerly toward the bedrooms.

Lori, who had taken a few minutes to put away the groceries in the kitchen and to explore the condo, was still changing when the others were on their way down the wooden stairs that led to the beach. She glanced around at the beautifully furnished bedroom she and Alex were going to share. The twin beds had light cotton spreads, and there were elegant Oriental-style dressing tables for each of them. The room, which had its own private bath, opened onto a high-fenced sundeck, with a terry-covered lounge chair strategically placed for sunbathing. The condo was even more luxurious than she had imagined, with its gleaming modern kitchen, the two spacious bedrooms, and a hot tub surrounded by blooming plants on the wooden deck overlooking the ocean.

Lori pulled a brush through her long, wheat-colored hair. If this was Clare Karlysle's *vacation* house, what was her Manhattan apartment like? Was this how *she* could live if she stayed in modeling and her career kept on going the same way? She shook her head and looked at herself in the mirror. Was it worth giving up the chance to have *this* kind of life, just because she didn't find it satisfying right now? At least she knew she was good at it.

Lori's thoughts were interrupted by the doorbell. Hastily, she zipped up her white shorts and pulled a blue top over her head. She ran barefoot to the door and stood there, hesitating. Who could it possibly be? She didn't know anybody in Hawaii.

"Hello," the young man said, when Lori finally opened the door. He was lounging barefoot against the trellis, his hands in the pockets of immaculate baggy white pants, a loose cotton shirt open to reveal a bare, deeply tanned chest. A shock of black hair swept across his forehead, and his dark, deep-set eyes were heavily lashed. He was in his middle twenties, Lori guessed. "I'm Kevin Duvall," he added. "You must be Lori Woodhouse."

"Oh, yes," Lori said. The person who had sent the flowers. But who was he? And how did he know who *she* was?

"Did you like them?" Kevin asked. "The flowers, that is."

"I . . . we loved them," Lori stammered, a blush creeping up her cheeks. "They're beautiful! Thank you."

"You're welcome," Kevin said, with an ela-
borate little bow. "I just came to add my own
personal welcome. I'm your neighbor." He
smiled, showing a row of even white teeth.
Two dimples appeared in his cheeks.

Lori felt herself relaxing a little under the
warmth of Kevin's smile. Well, that explained
it, then. But she still couldn't figure out how
he had known who she was.

He gestured with his head. "I'm staying in
the condo just down the hill." He smiled
again, charmingly. "It's so isolated around
here that neighbors get to know one another
pretty quickly."

Suddenly Lori remembered her manners.
"I . . . won't you come in?" she asked, opening
the door wider. "The others have gone down
to the beach, so I'm afraid you won't get to
meet them just now. But . . ."

"That's okay," Kevin said, stepping in and
shutting the door behind him. "Of course, I'd
like to meet them, too. But it's really *you* I
came to see, Lori." His eyes were on hers, deep
and hypnotic.

"Me?" Lori asked, stepping back in surprise. She could feel her face getting pinker
and pinker under Kevin's intense gaze, and
she felt a momentary flicker of fear. Neighbor
or no neighbor, why had she invited this

stranger into the house? And why in the world had she told him that she was here all by herself? She looked out the window toward the beach. She could see three figures far below, running across the white sand toward the water. If she had to scream now, they'd never hear her.

Kevin chuckled, the laughter rising deep in his throat. "Of course I came to see you," he said, giving her a warm, appraising glance. He followed her down the hall. "Clare Karlysle told me you were coming. In fact, she told me all about you. And when she showed me a picture, I knew I had to meet you."

"Oh," Lori said, some of her fear disappearing. If he was a friend of Clare's . . .

Kevin laughed as they went into the living room. "There's really no mystery about any of this, in case you're concerned. I've known Clare for years. We've . . . we've worked together, on occasion. I live in New York, actually—like you. I'm just here for the holidays."

"Oh, I see." Lori sat down on the sofa, relieved. She pulled her bare feet up and tucked them under her. "Well, I'm glad to meet a friend of Clare. She's a wonderful person."

Kevin glanced at her. "Yes, isn't she? She helps out a lot of new models.

Lori felt a twinge of guilt. Clare *had* helped her a great deal. And just look at the wonderful gift she had given her—a week at this luxurious condo! Was it fair to turn her back on her now, when the Cachet job would mean such a large commission for the agency? She dismissed the question from her mind. She wasn't going to think about that just now. "What kind of work do you do in New York?" she asked Kevin.

Kevin flashed her a crooked smile. "I'm in advertising," he said. He stood up and went to the window, looking down at the beach, hands in his pockets. "Are those your friends down there?"

"Yes." Lori got up to join him. The girls were walking up the beach now, wading knee-deep in the ocean.

"You were on your way to join them, weren't you?" Kevin asked. Without waiting for an answer, he reached casually for her hand. "Come on, I'll walk that way with you. I can get home from the beach."

For some reason, Lori felt as if she should protest. But she didn't. After all, he was their neighbor. And it had been very nice of him to send the flowers.

When Lori and Kevin caught up with them, the girls were gathered around a small pile of shells on the beach, chattering excitedly. They looked up as Lori approached, and Kit and Elaine scrambled to their feet, eyeing the newcomer curiously.

"Uh, hi," Lori said. "I'd like you to meet our neighbor, Kevin Duvall. Kevin, these are my friends Alex, Kit, and Elaine."

Kevin shook hands politely with each of them. "Welcome to Maui," he said, smiling easily. "I hope you have a pleasant stay."

"Oh, I'm sure we will," Kit said. Elaine held up a small pink shell, tightly spiraled and speckled with gold. "Can you tell us what this is?"

Kevin took it from her and studied it. "It's called a Hebrew cone," he said, handing it back. "You'll find lots of them around here. And in the shops, too. They make nice neck-laces, although the best ones are hard to find and expensive."

With a nod, Elaine put it into the pocket of her shorts. "Why pay for a necklace when I can pick it up off the beach?" she asked. She started off down the sand, her eyes on her feet. "I think I'll just look a little further," she said. "There might be some better ones down in this direction."

Kevin laughed. "Better watch out," he told the girls. "Beachcomber's fever can become a near fatal disease. People have been known to give up their families and their jobs just to live where they can see what wonderful things the tide brings in every day. There's no known treatment for it, I understand."

Kit tossed her blond hair out of her eyes. "Elaine's exactly the one to catch it, too," she said. "She's got more curiosity than the rest of us put together."

"Well, the beach is a good place for people who are curious about nature," Kevin said. He pointed toward the horizon. "For instance, if you look out toward the horizon early in the morning, especially on a windy day when the ocean is rough, you're likely to see a school of humpback whales. Sometimes you'll even see them slapping their tails on the water or blowing spume. It's quite a sight."

Lori looked out at the surf. There were plenty of people swimming to the south of them. Here, the beach was deserted. "Is it safe to swim here?" she asked.

"I'd watch out for the undertow at this spot," Kevin said. "Actually, there isn't anything around here that will harm you," he added, "—except for the jellyfish. They can sting pretty badly, but not fatally. Better *malama pono,* as the natives say."

"Malama pono?" Alex asked.

"Be careful," Kevin responded, with a quick grin. He looked down at his heavy gold wristwatch. "Well, I guess I'd better get back home. I put some charcoal into the barbecue, and it should be ready by now." He looked at the girls. "I'm having chicken, and there's plenty for everybody. Would you like to join me for dinner?"

Lori shook her head quickly, without looking at the others. "No, thanks," she said. "I think we're all too tired. We've been traveling for quite a while."

"Well, then," Kevin persisted, "how about tomorrow night? The Kapalu Bay Hotel is having a luau, and it ought to be fun. They put on quite a show. It's just like a feast in old Hawaii."

"Well . . ." For some reason, Lori felt hesitant. There was something about Kevin that made her feel uncomfortable, even though she couldn't put her finger on it. But Elaine, who had come back to the group with her hands full of shells, didn't hesitate at all.

"That sounds wonderful!" she said. "A genuine luau! We'll all have to go into town and buy muumuus to wear."

"You'll be right in style," Kevin said with a laugh. "All the women wear them. Well, then, I'll see you all tomorrow night." He turned away and scuffed through the deep sand toward a flight of stairs that went up the cliff.

"Wow," Kit said, staring after him. "He is *sharp*. And did you see the look he gave

Lori?"

"Wow and double wow," Elaine repeated, looking after Kevin. "Lorei, do good-looking guys like Kevin Duvall approach you often? He's exactly the kind of guy I'd love to find for a fling."

Lori colored. "I don't know what you mean," she said defensively. "He's just being nice, that's all. Listen, you guys, I'm getting hungry," she added. "I think it's time we went back and made a salad or something."

Kit put her arm around Lori's shoulders as they began to walk back along the beach toward the condo. The evening had faded into a purple twilight and Elaine and Alex were running ahead, laughing and splashing water at the seabirds that darted along the wet sand in front of them. "Well, Lori," she said, "you may be more self-confident than you were last year, and you're certainly more beautiful than ever. But one thing about you hasn't changed since our days at Glenwood High."

"What's that?" Lori asked, looking out at the tranquil ocean, faded now to a shade of deep pearl-gray.

"You're still afraid of guys."

Lori didn't answer. She was thinking of the easy way that she and Chris Farleigh had fallen in love. She had let herself be swept up in that relationship, although later she wasn't sure whether it was a choice she had consciously made for herself, or one that had been made for her, in some way she didn't understand. The same thing had happened just now. She wasn't sure she *wanted* to go to the luau tomorrow night with Kevin, but she had let herself be pulled along because the others wanted to do it. Was Kit right? Was it fear that held her back? Or was it the voice of cautious wisdom?

Lori felt a sudden confusion envelop her, almost as though a San Francisco fog had suddenly rolled over her in the midst of a clear Hawaiian twilight. What *should* she do with her life? How could she answer the questions that seemed to confront her from every side?

She looked up the gentle, sloping beach, trying to absorb the tranquility of the evening, hoping it would quiet her jangled thoughts. As she looked, she saw an old, gray-bearded man, shuffling along slowly at the high-tide mark, obviously a beachcomber. His clothes were ragged and unkempt, and he wore a tattered brown felt hat pulled down low over his ears. His pace was leisurely and unhurried, and even though his shoulders were stooped and he walked with a slight limp, he looked contented and peaceful.

Lori gazed at the old man. What would it be

like to live such a peaceful, unharried life, with no photographers yelling at her, no cameras pointed into her face, no deadlines to meet, no buses to catch? What would it be like to just sit in the sand and watch the sun set, or sit quietly on the rocks with her sketch pad, sketching the gulls and terns that dipped and whirled over the beach? For a moment, Lori almost found herself envying the old man.

Chapter Seven

The girls all slept until nearly eleven the next morning. "Ooh," Kit moaned as she came into the kitchen, rubbing her eyes with the back of her hand. "Jet lag. Where's the coffee?"

Perched on the bar stool at the counter with a towel wrapped around her still-damp hair, Elaine looked at her friend sympathetically. She'd only had to fly from the West Coast, while Kit and Lori had had a much longer trip. "How about a couple of hours in the sun instead?" she asked. "Lying on the beach slathered in suntan oil should be the ideal treatment for your jet lag."

"I don't know," Kit said, looking around blearily. She pushed the tousled hair off her forehead. "Give me a minute with my coffee, then I'll think about it."

Elaine watched as Kit stooped over, looking into the cupboard for the coffee they had bought the night before. She was wearing a pair of very short pink shorts and one of her old ruffled blouses that Elaine remembered so well. Her figure was voluptuous, even though it had been trimmed and firmed from all her dance classes. Still, there had always been a certain kind of almost childlike vulnerability about Kit that radiated through her sexiness, and she was easy and spontaneous in a way that Elaine admired and envied. Especially around boys, Kit had a knack for saying the right thing at the right time. Sometimes, it didn't seem fair that Elaine had to *work* at being relaxed and natural, while with Kit, being natural was the only way she could be.

"That's better," Kit said after a few minutes. She sat down beside Elaine, holding a steaming cup in her hands. She looked around. "Where are Lori and Alex? Out on the beach already?"

"They drove to the diving-supply store," Elaine explained. "Alex is interested in renting some snorkeling equipment and finding out about going on some dives."

Kit shuddered. "I think I'll stick to the top of the water," she said, shaking her head. "Or better yet, the sand. Putting on one of those masks makes me feel positively claustrophobic." She took another sip of coffee. "Have you noticed anything different about Alex?" she asked.

Elaine stared out the window at the ocean.

Fifty yards out, the surf was breaking, and she could see a small cluster of people with surfboards standing on the beach, watching while an instructor demonstrated several surfing techniques on the sand. "She doesn't quite seem the same, does she?" Elaine responded. "I noticed last night that she seems much more subdued, not as lively as she used to be."

Kit nodded. "I suppose it's because of Wes's death. She's so withdrawn, as if she doesn't really want to be around people."

"I wish there was something we could do to help her," Elaine said. "She's helped me so often, just by being Alex. But I don't know how. I'm really stumped." She pulled the towel off her head and began to rub her hair dry.

"I think this is something she's got to work out for herself," Kit said. Suddenly she put down her cup and stared at Elaine. "Elaine, what have you done to your hair? It's *red*!"

Elaine laughed self-consciously. "Oh, I just put a henna rinse on it this morning, that's all," she said. "I thought it would look better if there were some red highlights in it. It's always been such a *mousy* shade of brown."

She began to comb through it. "You sound as if you don't like it," she said apprehensively. "Is it too red?"

"No," Kit said, still staring. "It's going to look great once it's dry. I was just surprised, that's all. First green eyes, now auburn hair." She giggled. "Are you getting ready for your fling?"

"I guess so." Elaine looked out the window again. The cluster of student-surfers were trailing the instructor down the beach toward the water. On an impulse, she put down the comb and picked up the binoculars that were sitting on the end of the counter. Through the high-powered lenses, she could see that the instructor was very good-looking with blond hair and broad, muscular shoulders. With sudden decision she put down the binoculars.

"Come on," she said. "Let's put on our swimsuits and go down to the beach."

Kit picked up the binoculars and looked through them. "Ah-ha," she said with a laugh. "I see what you mean." She sighed and turned to follow Elaine. "For some reason, they don't seem to build them quite like that in New York."

The beach was pretty crowded by the time Elaine and Kit got there. "Gosh, where do all the people come from?" Kit asked, as they put down the Styrofoam cooler and spread their towels on the sand. "Last night, the beach was deserted."

Elaine pointed down toward the south. "I guess they come from the hotels," she said. "The Kapula Bay Hotel, where we're going tonight is just on the other side of that point, according to the map. The point is called Pu'u Keka'a," she added. "It's what the guidebook calls a spatter cone. I guess it used to be a little volcano or something like that." She took a deep breath and pulled off her white cotton cover-up, exposing her new bikini. And *exposing*, she thought wryly, was exactly the right word.

"If you do me," she bargained, opening a bottle of suntan oil, "I'll do you." Kit's eyes widened behind her sunglasses when she saw Elaine's new swimsuit. "My goodness," she marveled, staring at her friend. "That certainly is a . . . *striking* black bikini."

Elaine stretched out on her stomach as Kit leaned over her. "Do you like it?" she asked hesitantly. The only time she had worn such a skimpy bikini was when Brian Fitzgerald, her young boss at Orion Electronics, had invited her to dinner. Much to Elaine's dismay, they had wound up in Brian's hot tub, Elaine in a borrowed red bikini that had seemed to her nothing more than a handful of strings and a couple of pieces of fabric the size of theater tickets. This bikini was a little more modest, but not by much.

"Yeah, I like it. You look great," Kit replied. Her own swimsuit was a sleek, peacock-blue maillot with a plunging neckline. She finished with Elaine's back and opened the cooler, laughing a little as she offered Elaine a cold root beer. "Green eyes, auburn hair, and a tiny black bikini. What next?"

"Next, I hope," Elaine said, rolling over on her back and taking the soft drink from Kit, "is a *fling*."

"Hi," a deep male voice said. "I'll trade you a surfing lesson for a root beer."

Elaine sat up suddenly, her sunglasses slipping down her oily nose. Her first instinct was to pull on her cover-up, but she resisted it. Why had she bought a bikini if she was just going to cover it up? She looked up. The guy who was asking for the root beer was the same one she had seen through the binoculars. Close up, he was even more handsome than he had looked from the window.

"Sure," Elaine said, scrambling to open the cooler. "You can have a root beer. We have plenty. I'm not sure about the surfing lesson, though."

"Thanks," he said, squatting down beside Elaine and drinking his root beer in big gulps.

She noticed with some consternation that he appeared to be staring at her. "This really hits the spot," he added. His eyes, Elaine saw, were neon-blue, and they matched the zinc oxide he had smeared on his nose to keep off the sun.

Elaine looked away from his gaze with effort, wishing she could think of something to say. Kit, however, wasn't quite so tongue-tied.

"Hi," she said, in her usual friendly voice, holding out her hand. "My name's Kit. This is Elaine. We're here for the holidays."

"I'm Joe," the boy said. "Joe Kendall." He took Kit's hand briefly and then turned to Elaine. He held hers for a moment longer, as her face flamed red. "Are you staying at one of the hotels?" he asked.

Kit hesitated, and when Elaine didn't reply, she said, pointing, "No, we're staying in that condo up there."

"It must be nice not to have to stay in a hotel," Joe said. "They're full of middle-aged tourists." He laughed. "I work in one some-times."

Elaine managed to find her tongue. "You do?" she asked.

Joe jerked his thumb over his shoulder. "The Kapalua Bay Hotel," he said. "Just on the other side of Black Rock."

"Oh, you mean Pu'u Keka'a," Elaine said, remembering what she had read. "The guidebook says that it's a spatter cone."

"Yeah, well, I wouldn't know about spatter cones," Joe responded. "The people around here call it Black Rock." He grinned and winked at her. "Because it is. Black, I mean. I don't know too much about natural history and stuff. That's for tour guides and teachers. Myself, I'm into surfing."

Elaine felt herself flushing. She had a feeling that Joe Kendall wasn't exactly an intellectual heavyweight. But he certainly was good-looking. Seen at close range, his biceps bulged and his muscular chest narrowed down compactly to a small waist.

"Well," she said, trying not to stare, "surfing looks like fun. Maybe I will try it."

Joe glanced at her bikini. "Well, anytime," he said. "Just let me know. You can always find me around here. Thanks for the root beer." He stood up and ambled away toward the water.

"What arrogance!" Elaine exclaimed when he was out of earshot.

"What a hunk," Kit said, looking after him. She turned to Elaine. "I thought you were looking for a fling."

"Well, I am," Elaine said. "But I had in mind someone a little more . . ." She stopped,

90

searching for words.

"A little more up to your intellectual speed, maybe?" Kit asked, regarding her closely.

"Well, yes," Elaine admitted. "I suppose so."

"Listen, Elaine," Kit said earnestly, "if it's a fling you want, with no commitments, doesn't it make sense to go for the body, not the mind?"

"Well, maybe," Elaine conceded grudgingly. "But I did hope that . . ."

"Come on," Kit interrupted her, getting to her feet and holding out her hand. "I'm beginning to broil. Why don't we continue this discussion in the water?" She giggled. "Your suit is guaranteed against shrinkage, isn't it?"

When Lori and Alex came home from their morning in town, they brought with them presents for everyone—four brightly flowered muumuus.

"We couldn't resist," Lori said, as the girls, laughing and chattering, began to get dressed to go to the Kapalua hotel for the luau. "Around here, everybody wears them, tourists and natives alike."

"Well, at least we don't have to worry about showing too much of anything," Kit said. "Even our feet." She slipped into a huge, voluminous black muumuu spattered with pink hibiscus blossoms. "Nobody can accuse us of being underdressed."

Elaine giggled. "That's exactly why the missionaries made the native women wear these things," she told them, remembering what the guidebook had said. "They were scandalized when they saw the grass skirts and skimpy tops that the women were wearing, and they bought bolts of the brightest cloth they could find in order to cover them up, from their chins to their toes." She turned around in front of the mirror. "It does leave a *lot* to the imagination."

"Well, I can't say that I'd like to wear one of these as a regular affair," Kit said. She bent over to put on a pair of sandals. "I like to leave a little less to the imagination. But it's okay for one night, anyway."

Lori came back from the hallway, where she had gone to answer the doorbell. She was carrying a large white box in her hands, and her cheeks were stained pink. Elaine couldn't tell whether she was pleased or embarrassed.

"Don't tell me. Let me guess," Alex remarked, pulling her magenta muumuu over her head. "It's from Kevin Duvall, isn't it?"

"Yes," Lori admitted in a low voice. She put the box on the bed and opened it to the sound of excited "oohs."

Inside were four exquisite orchids, each a different color. Lori and Elaine pinned theirs to their dresses; Alex put hers in her hair, and Kit fastened hers to her wrist, prom-style. Full of anticipation, they climbed into the car and set off to meet Kevin at the hotel.

The luau was taking place outside, on the wide hotel patio, ringed on three sides by lush green tropical plants and open on the fourth side to the beach and the ocean, where the sun was setting in a pool of rich, radiant pinks and lavenders.

Looking very handsome in a white dinner jacket, Kevin was waiting for the girls at a table he had reserved for the five of them overlooking the ocean. He stood up when they arrived, and Elaine watched enviously as he pulled out a white wicker chair for Lori, gesturing for her to sit next to him. Lori was so lucky, she thought. Why couldn't she meet someone as intelligent and charming as Kevin? *That* would be the perfect fling.

"Okay, now, everybody watch," Kevin said, directing their attention toward the point of black rock that rose twenty feet above the ocean, to their right. Flickering in the early twilight, torches were lit all the way to the point. "It's about to begin."

"What's about to begin?" Kit asked, nibbling on the sushi that Kevin had ordered for hors d'oeuvres. Sashimi turned out to be little rolls of raw fish in a rice-and-seaweed blanket.

"You'll see," Kevin said mysteriously. "Just watch."

As the crowd looked on, a native Hawaiian boy, his shoulders heavy with leis, clambered up to the top of Black Rock. For a long moment he stood there, motionless against the last rays of the setting sun, muted Hawaiian guitars playing in the background. Then, with a dramatic gesture, he tore the leis from around his neck and flung them into the water below. As the crowd held its breath in silent suspense, he raised his arms over his head and arched into a perfect dive, cutting into the ocean twenty feet below almost without a splash. The crowd burst into instantaneous applause.

"According to tradition," Kevin explained to them as the boy climbed out of the water, "Black Rock is the place where the soul leaps into the afterworld. They call it *leina a ka 'uhane.* A 'soul's leap.' When a person is ready to die, they say, his soul leaves his body and wanders around. If all his earthly obligations have been fulfilled, the soul finds its way to Black Rock. There it is taken by the gods, and at that moment, the person is free to die.

The boy's plunge into the ocean is a symbol of the leap of the soul into the hands of the gods."

The girls listened, fascinated, to Kevin's story.

"What a wonderful story!" Elaine exclaimed. "And what a beautiful place!"

She looked around. Over their heads, hundreds of softly luminous Japanese lanterns swung in the breeze, and torches lined the beachfront. A group of Polynesian dancers, skin the color of Alex's, swayed gracefully to the strumming of a guitar, dancing a *hula*. The fragrance of roast pig filled the air, coming from the deep trenches dug in the sand beneath them, where suckling pigs were being cooked over live coals, covered with layers of banana leaves. On tables behind them an incredible buffet was set out, with huge, steaming platters of *mahimahi, teriyaki*, shrimp, *kiawe* chicken, and fish broiled in some sort of green leaf. There was the unmistakable purple *poi*, breadfruit, pineapple, and guava. Another table was piled high with all sorts of cakes, mousses, and pies.

"Don't look now," Kit whispered to Elaine, "but somebody very cute is staring at you. He's over there, by the dessert table."

Elaine looked around, trying to act natural.

Joe Kendall was watching her with a rakish grin, one eyebrow raised. Tonight he was dressed in a flowered shirt and a pair of white chinos, and she had to admit that he *was* remarkably good-looking. He was obviously working, because he wore a green towel looped around his waist and he had a tray under his arm.

"Who is that?" Alex asked Kit, seeing the glances that Elaine and Joe were exchanging.

"A guy we met on the beach today," Kit explained. "He might be a candidate for Elaine's super fling."

As if on cue, Joe sauntered over to the table. "I just wanted to say hi," he said to Elaine, "and thanks again for the root beer."

"Don't mention it," Elaine said nervously. She felt Kit's foot kicking her ankle, and she introduced Joe to the others.

"I'm working now," Joe told her, "but I get off at ten. If you're still around, maybe we can do some dancing. How about it?"

Elaine hesitated, then nodded. Kit was right. It you were looking for something temporary, did it matter whether the guy had a degree in electrical engineering from MIT?

When it was time to eat, the girls made several trips to the buffet tables, trying everything until they were stuffed.

"Now I know why they wear these muumuus here," Elaine said to Kit, pushing her chair away from the table. "You can eat anything you want and not have to worry about bulges."

After dinner, Lori and Kevin wandered off in the direction of the beach. Kit and Alex went inside to watch the floor show, a magician from L.A., and Joe came over to ask Elaine to dance. When he put his arms around her and pulled her close, Elaine decided that Joe was definitely the right candidate for a fling. The feeling that she got was meltingly *physical.*

Chapter Eight

Alex got up early the next morning, before any of the others were awake and, grabbing her camera, went for a walk to Kula Falls, a little over a mile from the condominium. She'd never really *liked* getting up with the sun, but she'd gotten into the habit a long time ago, since the pool was always empty at 7 AM, and the early-morning habit was a hard one to break. The minute the birds began to chirp, she was awake, and here, with such *noisy* birds, it was impossible to sleep once the sun began to touch the tops of the palm trees.

The trail led steeply upward across a rough lava flow, between nearly vertical walls. In places, the lava was broken and sharp, almost splintery, and Alex was glad that she had worn her jogging shoes. Beneath the trail, the stream flowed musically among mossy boulders, and clumps of green ferns grew thick in the cool, damp shade.

As she walked along the narrow trail, Alex thought about what had happened the night before. Watching Joe try his tricks on Elaine and seeing Kevin Duvall making such a smooth, practiced play for Lori, Alex had become even more convinced of the wisdom of her decision to stay on the sidelines and let others play the romance game. Sure, romance looked like fun—in the beginning. It was always easy in the beginning to laugh and flirt and be charming.

But it was only a matter of time before everything got difficult, and in the end there was always the pain of loss, no matter what. In fact, last night hadn't been very much fun for Alex, because she could see so clearly where her friends were heading, and she wanted to warn them. But she hadn't. Everybody had to learn from their own mistakes. She had learned that the higher your expectations, the more likely you were to be disappointed. From that point of view, it was better not to have any expectations—and that meant not having any relationships.

Alex finally reached the falls at the top of the trail, where the water cascaded over a broken fault nearly thirty feet over her head. For a moment she stood beneath the cool, wet spray, feeling it splash against her skin. It made her feel alive and energetic, as if it were a source of strength. She didn't feel that way very often these days, she had to admit.

After a few minutes, Alex got out her camera and took several photos of the falls and the fragrant lehua blossoms that were scattered like red puffballs through the open glade. Fuschia grew wild here, too. Garlands of delicate purple and pink blooms festooned the trees. When Alex started back down the trail, she felt rested and somehow rejuvenated. And in spite of the fact that she enjoyed being with her friends, she was glad she had come alone. She had needed some time to sort out her feelings.

When she got back to the condo, she found Lori sitting on the deck in her swimsuit, reading and getting some sun.

"Have you been for a walk?" Lori asked, looking up from her book.

Alex nodded. She sat down on one of the plastic deck chairs and took off her jogging shoes. "I went up to the falls," she said. "It was beautiful."

"Yes, Kevin said it was a pretty trail," Lori said. She looked out across the ocean, and then she asked, "What do you think of Kevin?"

Alex hesitated. "He seems like a nice guy," she said after a moment. "And he's obviously interested in you. What happened last night?"

Lori blushed. "Oh, nothing much," she said.

"You were gone for a long time," Alex persisted. "Did you walk down the beach?"

"Not very far. Actually, we just found a place to sit on the sand, and we talked for a while." She laughed in embarrassment and looked down at her book. "Then we came back."

Alex smiled. Lori hadn't changed very much in some ways, in spite of the New York polish she seemed to have acquired. She was still more secretive than any of the others. With Kit, for example, it was easy to know what she was thinking. She was always ready to tell you—even when you weren't sure that you wanted to know. Lori had never shared her feelings very easily.

"How do you like New York?" Alex asked.

"I like it," Lori answered. "I mean, I like the city a lot. There's always something exciting going on, plays and movies and music. And people—even ordinary people on the street—wear the most incredible clothes. But..."

"But what?" Alex prodded.

Lori shrugged. "Oh, I don't know," she said vaguely. "It isn't the city that troubles me. Sometimes I think it's my work. Or maybe . . ." Her voice trailed off. She shrugged again. "I don't know," she said, her voice sounding closed off.

Alex stood up. Lori obviously wasn't going to talk. "Well," she said, looking at her watch. "It's nearly nine-thirty. Maybe we can go snorkeling. The people at the dive shop said that the boat goes out to the reef every morning at ten-thirty. What about it?"

Lori was already deep in her book. "I don't think so," she muttered. "I'm going to read for a while and then go to the beach."

"Okay," Alex said cheerfully and went back inside, to the bedrooms. In the room they shared, Kit and Elaine were still just shapeless heaps under the blankets. Kit stirred.

"How about going snorkeling with me this morning?" Alex asked. "The boat leaves in an hour, so if you're interested, we'd better hurry." She turned the wand on the blinds to open them.

Kit pulled her pillow over her head and then looked out, squinting against the light. She had one foot out from under the covers, and Alex saw that she was wearing her favorite red harem pajamas. "Good grief, Alex," Kit moaned, pulling the pillow over her head again. "What are you doing up so *early*? It's practically dawn."

"Dawn?" Alex repeated. "It's not early. The

sun's been up for nearly four hours. It's nine-thirty. Back at Northwestern, I'd have been in classes for an hour and a half by now."

"But you're *not* back at Northwestern," Elaine pointed out, stretching. She yawned. "It's snowing back at Northwestern, and you're *here*, on vacation. Can't you relax, even on vacation? Snorkeling is hard work, Alex. Can't it at least wait until after lunch?"

"Yes, but the water is calmer in the morning," Alex protested, looking out the window. "After lunch, the trade winds start to blow, and the water ripples so that you can't see very well."

"Yes, but I can't see very well *before* lunch," Kit remarked. "Especially when I'm on vacation." She sat up and rubbed the sleep out of her eyes. "What happened to the assignment you gave yourself? I thought you were just going to lie in the sun and relax. And here you are, talking about snorkeling already."

Alex laughed. "I suppose you're right. It's just that I don't want to waste any time. We won't be here that long and life is so short and . . ."

She stopped suddenly, thinking of Noodle. Life had been *very* short for him. Yet Noodle had always seemed to live every moment to the fullest. And Wes—even though he had been the most fiercely competitive person she had ever known, Wes had also been the most fun-loving, always ready to relax and laugh. He had once told Alex that she was wound as tightly as the mainspring of a watch, and if she didn't look out, some day she would snap.

But Wes wasn't the only one who had poked fun at her tensely competitive nature. Danny, her boyfriend before Wes, used to call her "Supergirl." "Faster than a speeding bullet," he would say. So her habit of expecting a lot of herself—and of the people she loved— went back a long way.

"Don't think I'm up to snorkeling this morning," Elaine was mumbling inarticulately as she turned her face to the wall and burrowed back down under the covers. "Not after last night."

"Ah-ha," Kit said. "And just what time did you get in last night?"

"I don't know," Elaine said, in a muffled voice. "I didn't look at the clock."

"Well, *I* did," Kit said pointedly. "It was after two."

"It was?" Elaine yawned and rolled over. "I guess I lost track of time."

"You see," Kit said with satisfaction, "it doesn't require brains to have a fling. I'll bet..."

Kit's voice faded behind Alex as she left the

room and went down the hall. She might have known better than to try to get Kit out of bed before noon. Early mornings had always been Kit's downfall. Alex wondered how she managed early classes at Juilliard. But Elaine had always been an early riser, like Alex. It was a little disappointing to . . .

Frowning, Alex caught herself up short. She was doing it again—just when she promised herself she'd never expect *anything* from anyone. She sighed and went to get her swimsuit and a towel. It was almost ten o'clock. She still had time to catch the boat out to the reef for the snorkeling trip.

The reef was spectacular. The water was a clear blue-green and the sea anemone and starfish that encrusted the coral a few feet below were like rare, colorful flowers in a beautiful garden. Schools of lemon fish drifted lazily through the warm water, while hermit crabs and lobsters scuttled among the coral. Now and then, Alex could see eels peering out of crevices in the reef, and fat, round porcupine fish hung in mid-water like spiny balloons, manta rays sliding dreamily around them. She spent nearly three hours in the water, and she was sorry when it was time to get back on the boat. When she was in the water, looking at the spectacular sights on the reef, she didn't have to think about anything in particular. She could just relax and enjoy herself, letting go of the tension that made her feel tight and anxious inside.

After the boat returned to the marina, Alex wandered around the docks for a while, looking at the sailboats, imagining what it would be like to sail to some distant, exotic port, leaving all of her troubles behind.

When she got back to the condo, Lori was out on the beach, and Kit and Elaine were stretched out on their stomachs on the deck, nibbling at the sandwiches they had made for lunch and now and then basting each other lazily with suntan oil. Elaine, wearing her new skimpy bikini, was looking a little sunburned, in spite of the oil. Rock music blared from the radio.

"How was snorkeling?" Elaine asked, glancing up sleepily. "Did you see any sharks?"

"No sharks," Alex said. She leaned over and turned the radio down. "But there were plenty of turtles and eels and manta rays."

"Yuck," Kit shuddered. She was eating a liverwurst sandwich. "I hate eels. They're like snakes, all slimy and creepy. And I'll bet they bite."

"They may look creepy, but they're certainly not slimy," Alex protested, sitting on the rail. "And they don't bite—at least, not any more than two-legged creeps do," she added, with a laugh. Kit nearly choked on her liverwurst sandwich, and Elaine turned red. Alex wondered if they were thinking of Joe Kendall.

At that moment, the doorbell rang. Kit and Elaine looked too comfortable to budge, so Alex climbed off the rail to answer it.

Outside the door stood a boy in a brown uniform with a badge marked TELEGRAPH SERVICE. "I have a telegram for Mr. Alex Enomoto," he said, reading the address.

"That's me," Alex said, with a laugh. She was used to people thinking that Alex was a boy's name. "Honest," she said. "It's short for Alexandra."

The telegraph boy regarded her skeptically. "If you say so," he said, handing her the chewed stub of a pencil. "Sign here."

Alex scrawled her name and took the telegram, turning it over worriedly in her fingers. Who would be sending a telegram to her here—unless it was some sort of bad news? Her mind immediately flew to Stephanie, off on her skiing trip in the mountains with Rick. Had there been an accident?

Her fingers trembling a little, Alex ripped open the envelope. Her eyes widened when she saw the name at the bottom of the telegram. The telegram was from her old boyfriend Danny!

ARRIVING MAUI TOMORROW ON FRIEND'S BOAT
STOP LOVE TO SEE YOU IF YOU'LL COME OUT OF
THE WATER LONG ENOUGH STOP MERRY
CHRISTMAS STOP DANNY.

Danny was coming to Maui? She couldn't
believe it. Sure, she'd scribbled a note at the
bottom of the Christmas card she'd sent a
couple of weeks ago, mentioning something
about going to Hawaii with Lori and the
others for the holidays. But she certainly
hadn't expected *this!*

She leaned against the wall and read the
telegram again, smiling. She could almost
hear Danny's cheerful voice in the words,
printed so impersonally on the yellow paper,
and a vision of his sunny face came into her
mind—high cheekbones, eyes as aquamar-
ine as the water she had swum in this morning, hair streaked by the sun. He was always
brown from spending hours in the outdoor
pool, and four inches taller than she, just tall
enough so that her shoulder tucked under
the curve of his arm. They had been close for
so long, and Alex had loved him deeply. But
after a while, without either of them noticing

it, they had begun to drift apart—until finally, when Wes came into her life, it had been easy to let go of Danny. They had broken up just in time, she had always thought, while they still had good feelings about each other.

Easy to let go. No, that wasn't exactly true, Alex told herself, closing her eyes. It hadn't been easy to let Danny go. It had hurt a lot. And she could remember some of it so clearly, like the night that Danny and Stephanie had spent together in the woods, when she was convinced that the two of them had . . .

Elaine and Kit came into the living room, laughing uproariously at something. They stopped when they saw Alex leaning against the wall, the telegram in her hand.

"What is it, Alex?" Elaine asked anxiously. "Is everything okay?"

Alex looked up, slightly dazed. "I guess so," she said, jarred back to the present. "I mean, it depends on how you look at it."

"Well, what *is* it?" Kit asked, coming over and putting her arm around her. "What's going on?"

"Danny's coming."

"Danny?" Kit and Elaine said in unison. They stared at Alex. "DANNY? Coming to Maui?"

Alex nodded and handed them the telegram. While they were reading it, she went into the kitchen and pulled the makings for a grilled-cheese sandwich out of the refrigerator.

"Well?" Kit said expectantly, putting the telegram on the counter and climbing up on one of the bar stools.

"Well what?" Alex said. She buttered a slice of whole-wheat bread, then dropped it, butter side down, on the floor. She buttered another slice and put it in a skillet on the stove and turned on the heat.

"*You* know what," Kit said, propping her chin on her hands. "Are you glad he's coming? I mean, how do you feel about it?"

"Sure I'm glad," Alex replied, putting a slice of cheese on top of the bread. She buttered another slice and put it on top of the cheese, trying to make her voice sound cool. "Danny and I were lucky. When we broke up, we managed to stay friends. It's always good to see a friend, isn't it?" She went to the refrigerator to get the milk and a handful of carrot and celery sticks.

Elaine glanced at her shrewdly. "Just friends?" She stood beside Alex and began to make another sandwich. "While you've got the skillet out, I might as well have one, too," she added.

"Just friends," Alex said firmly. She poured a glass of milk, slopping some of it down the

110

side of the glass, and then flipped the sandwich over in the skillet so that the other side could brown.

"Well, maybe that will change when he gets here," Kit suggested with a smile. "I always did think that you and Danny were a perfect couple. I mean, you always just seemed to *belong* together, and Hawaii is such a romantic place. Maybe you'll . . ."

"And maybe we won't," Alex snapped. She slapped her grilled cheese sandwich onto a plate. She had managed to leave it in the skillet too long and one side was burned. "Danny and I had a good thing going—once. I don't intend to start it up again." *Or any other relationship,* she added to herself.

Kit gave her a knowing grin. "Okay, okay." She held up both hands. "You don't need to get all steamed up and nervous about it."

"Steamed up? Who's getting steamed up?" Alex demanded. She sat down at the table to eat her sandwich and then got up again. She'd forgotten the glass of milk she had already poured. "And what makes you think I'm nervous?"

"Oh, nobody's steamed up," Kit corrected herself hastily, staring at the burned sandwich on Alex's plate. "And nobody's nervous, either."

Alex sat down. She looked at her plate, then

up at Elaine. "Elaine," she said, in a meek voice, "would you mind handing me the carrot and celery sticks I left beside the sink?"

With a grin, Elaine brought her the vegetables.

"Oh, yes, and would you get the salt, too, please?" Alex added. "I left it on the stove."

And then all three of them dissolved in helpless laughter.

Chapter Nine

Lori came back from the beach and sat out alone on the deck, watching the gulls chase one another through the clear air. Farther out, a brown pelican flew low, just skimming the surface of the water. The birds looked so free, Lori thought, moving through the air without a care in the world. She watched them enviously.

Lori had thought that after she graduated, *she* would have that kind of freedom. She could make her own rules, set her own boundaries. The world would be hers to enjoy. But it wasn't working out that way. Everything in her life was complicated. If she took the modeling contract with Cachet, things would get even *more* complicated. How could she be free to do what she wanted to do if she had to sign a long-term contract? It was almost like selling herself.

Lost in thought, Lori only dimly heard the

phone ring. On what must have been the third or fourth ring, she got up to answer it.

"Hi, Lori. It's Kevin," a rich, deep voice said on the other end of the line.

Lori sat down on the floor with the receiver. "Hi, Kevin," she said, thinking about the night before. Was *he* thinking about it, too? She began to feel warm, so she stood up and pulled the chain on the ceiling fan, then sat down again.

Actually, not much had happened, but while they were sitting together on the beach he had kissed her with a passion that had taken her by surprise—and awakened a surprising response in her. She hadn't felt that way since Chris, and those days seemed like a very long time ago. Remembering Kevin's kisses now, she felt a sharp flicker of the same passion. Taking a deep breath, she tried to make her voice sound normal.

"What are you doing today?" she asked him. Then she blushed and bit her tongue. Would he think that was a leading question? That she was hinting that she wanted to be included in whatever he was doing?

"Not very much, actually," Kevin admitted. "Just relaxing in the sun with some ad copy I brought with me." He laughed. "In some jobs, you never stop working, you know. You just pack up the desk and take it with you."

Lori sighed. "Yes, I know," she said. She was beginning to feel that *she* hadn't really left her job behind. But Kevin didn't sound bothered by having to work. He sounded as if he actually *enjoyed* it.

"I was calling to see if you wanted to do something this afternoon," Kevin said. "Like maybe play tennis or golf. Or we could go sailing. Residents of these condos have special privileges at the club and the marina, you know."

Lori thought quickly. A part of her wanted to be with Kevin, but which part? She couldn't play tennis or golf, and she didn't really want to go sailing. In fact, there was another part of her that wanted to spend the day doing *her* thing, not somebody else's. She opened her mouth, and to her own surprise, heard her voice saying, "Thanks, but I think I'm going to do some sketching today."

"Oh." There was a distinct note of regret in Kevin's voice. "I can't talk you into it?" he asked. "The golf course is the best on Maui, and we could get a cart, if you don't feel like walking. And the tennis courts are absolutely super."

"No, thanks," Lori said, thinking how nice it would be to walk up the beach all by herself and find a quiet spot to sketch. "I'd really rather . . ."

"Or we could get a sailboat," Kevin went on, as if she hadn't spoken. "The marina has some very nice ones for rent. We could get a Hobie cat, if you're into strenuous sailing, or a keel boat, if you just want to sit and look beautiful." He paused. "Not that you don't look absolutely beautiful all the time," he added smoothly.

Lori took a deep breath, thinking about what Kit had said. Was she afraid of guys? Or was this feeling just a natural desire to be alone? She couldn't be sure. But the longer she talked with Kevin, the more she wanted to be by herself today. "Thanks all the same, Kevin," she said. "But I think I'll spend the afternoon alone."

"Well, okay," Kevin said reluctantly. There was no mistaking the surprise in his tone. He probably wasn't used to getting turned down. "I've got to fly to Honolulu tomorrow," he said, "but I'll call you after that," he added. "Why don't you start thinking about what you'd like to do."

"Well, okay," Lori said, feeling slightly trapped, "but . . ."

"No buts," Kevin said firmly. "I'll see you the day after tomorrow."

After she had hung up, Lori went into the bedroom and pulled on a pair of purple shorts and a white T-shirt. She could hear Elaine and Kit giggling hysterically in the next room. Then there was a breathless squeal and a dull thud that sounded like a pillow hitting the wall, followed by more squeals and a couple of *thwacks*. Obviously, Elaine and Kit were having a pillow fight.

Before they could discover her and get her to join in, she scribbled a note on a pad saying that she was going to the beach, took her sketch pad, and started out.

As she walked north along Kaanapali Beach, Lori discovered that the seashore became much rockier. Unlike the beach farther south, where the hotels screened the sand with a curtain of steel and glass, this area seemed wild and primitive. Here there was no outer barrier reef to protect the shore from the waves, and the surf was free to pound it, sending fountains of seawater breaking high into the air. Inland from the rocky edge of the water, Lori could see a wide white sand beach that rose up sharply, edged at the back by a broken line of low sand dunes. Many of the dunes had solidified, forming interesting silhouettes that cast strange shadows in the sun's strong light.

When she grew tired of looking into the tide pools, Lori carried her sketch pad up to the dunes and found a place where she could sit cross-legged in the sand, sheltered from the sun by an overhanging cliff. She began to draw rapidly, doing quick practice sketches of the shoreline and the wheeling birds. She wanted to capture the wild, desolate feeling of the place, the feeling that seemed to awaken a strange yearning in her.

At first she felt awkward, because she hadn't been sketching much lately. But after a few minutes, her fingers and her wrist loosened up, and she felt some of the old freedom and spontaneity that she used to feel when she drew. When she felt really comfortable with her pencil, she began to sketch the life immediately around her, the clumps of sea oats and goldenrod fanning gracefully out of the sand, the tiny sand creatures that scuttled across the face of the dunes, leaving feathery trails behind them, the sculpted shapes of the dunes, as shadowed and mysterious as ancient pyramids. Here, away from the tourists' automobiles and the hotels and shops, Lori could almost imagine that she was completely alone on the island.

She was working so intently that she didn't hear the sand crunch behind her until a shadow fell across her sketch pad. Startled, she looked up, shading her eyes against the sun. The man who stood there was the beachcomber Lori had seen a couple of days earlier, searching the beach for shells and driftwood.

"That's very good," the old man said, in a gravelly voice. "You're talented, Lori Woodhouse."

"How do you know my name?" Lori asked, in amazement.

The old man's face creased in a smile. "No magic," he said."You've signed your drawing. I just read your signature."

Above the man's long, unkempt gray beard, his cheeks were deeply seamed and furrowed, and his stern eyebrows were gray and craggy. Today, he was leaning on a walking stick, carved with what looked like a peculiar bird's head with a pronounced beak. But in spite of the man's age, his blue eyes were still sharp, and he looked at her with a probing intensity that made Lori shift uncomfortably in the sand. She felt as if he could see right through her. And yet she somehow wasn't afraid, for behind the intensity she sensed a strong kindliness and an unexpected sympathy.

"You *do* have talent, Lori Woodhouse," he repeated.

Lori looked down at the sketch pad. The pencil sketch of a gull sailing above the dunes was bold and vigorous, but still, what could an old beachcomber know about art? "Do I?" she asked, speaking more to herself than to the old man. "I'd like to think so — but I'm not sure."

"Why not?" The old man put his stick down and squatted on his heels beside her, picking a stalk of sea oats to chew on. His nearly white hair straggled untidily over the collar of his blue-denim work shirt, which he wore with the sleeves rolled up. Lori could see that the knees of his worn jeans had been patched several times, and his sneakers were stained and frayed. Altogether, he looked pretty disreputable. Obviously, he was the kind of beach bum that Kevin had told them about the other day — somebody who lived on practically nothing, who did nothing all day but look for whatever the tide had brought in. And yet there was something about his piercing blue eyes, something in his voice that made him seem different.

"Oh, I don't know," Lori sighed, in answer to his question. "I...I guess I don't have a whole lot of self-confidence."

Startled, she put down her pencil. Why had she said something as personal and honest as *that* to someone she didn't even know? To this dirty old beachcomber, who probably lived in a shack with a metal roof someplace behind the dunes. All her life, Lori had been a very private person who kept her most personal thoughts and feelings to herself, and she didn't think she was going to change now that she was growing up. She loved Elaine and Alex and Kit, but she had never understood how they could share so much of themselves with one another. No matter how much she cared for them, even they didn't know what was *really* going on inside her.

"You're very young," the old man remarked quietly, gazing out toward the ocean, his hair ruffling in an offshore breeze that had just sprung up. "People say that it's easy to be young. I don't agree. I think it's harder to be young than it is to be old." He poked gently at a little crab that had scuttled near the frayed toe of his sneakers. "When you're young," he added thoughtfully, "so many things demand your attention at once that it becomes very difficult to focus on what you really want to do. It's as if you are a juggler, and you have a dozen balls in the air at one time."

For an instant, Lori stared at the man in surprise. How could he have known so precisely what was in her mind?

"Yes, that's it," she blurted out. "I feel as if I can't do all of the things that are expected of me—and still do what I *want* to do. And the most ironic part of the whole thing is that these days I'm *doing* exactly what I always thought I wanted to do." She looked down at her sketch pad again. "Only it turns out that there's something else I want to do even more," she added. The words came out in a tumbling rush, surprising her with their intensity. She had known how she felt. She just hadn't known how much it mattered.

"And what is it that you're doing these days that you always thought you wanted to do?" the old man asked.

"I'm a model," Lori said, "in New York."

"Some people would think that you lead an exciting life," the man said.

"Sometimes it is exciting, but a lot of the time it's just plain boring," Lori admitted. "I spend most of my time standing in front of somebody's camera."

The old man turned to look at her, squinting a little in the bright afternoon sun. He scrutinized her closely. "Yes, I can see why people would want to capture your face," he said finally. "You have a very beautiful face." He paused. "But your face is only a part of you. There's more to you than just the outside."

"Yes, but nobody seems to realize that!" Lori burst out excitedly. What the old man was saying was exactly what she had been thinking for the last couple of days. "They *only* want my face! When I'm modeling, I know that they only want the *outside* of me. They only want to look at me, not *know* me!

Sometimes when I'm working I feel like...like I'm not a person. I'm just a puppet, and somebody else is pulling the strings, making me walk and bend and move the way they want me to walk and bend and move."

She took a deep, steadying breath. She thought she might start crying but she felt *relieved* finally saying out loud what she'd been thinking for so long. Out here on this windswept beach, four thousand miles from her home and her job, she had a strange feeling she could say anything to this old man she would never see again, an old man whose name she didn't even know. It was on the tip of her tongue to ask his name when he spoke again.

"So why do you keep on doing what you're doing?" the man asked calmly, watching a plover dart along the sand. "If you don't enjoy modeling, why don't you simply get out of it and do what you really want to do?"

Lori looked out to sea. Far out, a cloud bank was forming, a line of hazy gray against the blue-gray of the ocean. "I don't know," she said. When she tried to think about the future, it seemed as hazy as that mass of clouds. "I mean, I'm making a lot of money, and that's nice." She thought briefly about how good it was to be able to treat her friends to a Hawaiian vacation, and what it would be like to live like this all the time. "If I stay in modeling I'll be able to live very comfortably and buy fashionable clothes and a new car and travel all over the world and . . ."

"And be a tourist all your life. Is that it?" The old man completed her sentence. He chuckled, and the corners of his moustache turned up. "When the world isn't looking at you through the lens of a camera, you'd be looking at the world through the lens of a camera."

Lori sighed. When he put it that way, she knew it wasn't at all what she wanted. "No," she said quietly. "I don't want to be a tourist all my life. I want to be able to *do* something, something that I'm proud of."

The old man leaned over and tapped her sketch pad with his gnarled fingers. "Then why don't you do more of this?" he asked.

Lori felt as if their conversation had come full circle. "Because I don't know whether I have any talent or not," she said. "Because I don't think I could support myself with my art. Because . . ."

"Because you're afraid?" the old man prompted gently.

Lori fell silent, staring out at the ocean. The clouds were forming swiftly now, and a cooler breeze blew toward the beach, bringing with it a definite hint of rain. "I just don't know," she replied with a sigh. "I just don't know." It was the same question she had asked herself about Kevin. How could you tell the difference between being afraid and being cautious?

The old man stood up and picked up his cane. For a moment he stood there, looking down at Lori's drawing. "You do have talent," he said finally. "I can see it. But you're the one who has to acknowledge it. And once you've acknowledged it, you have to decide what you're going to do about it."

While she sat there, open-mouthed with surprise, he turned without a backward glance and ambled down the dune. In another moment he was gone, and the first drops of rain began to fall.

Chapter Ten

"Is it still raining?" Elaine asked plaintively, from the depths of her pillow. It would just be my luck, she thought. *The day that Joe Kendall, Hawaiian Hunk, invited me to go bodysurfing with him, it* would *naturally rain.*

"Why don't you look and see?" Kit asked from the other bed. Her head was a mass of ringlets the color of ripe wheat. She leaned precariously across the space between the beds and yanked the pillow off Elaine's head. "Guess what!" she crowed. "Sunshine!"

Elaine sat up. "Oh, wonderful!" she said, clapping her hands and pointing out the window, where the sun was painting the glistening palm trees with gold. "The three of us can go bodysurfing!"

"What's this 'three' stuff, kemo-sabi?" Kit asked in surprise. She climbed out of bed and shucked her harem pajamas, for a moment admiring her newly tanned self in the mirror. "I thought this was strictly a one-girl, one-boy party. Just you and your passionate friend Joe."

"Well, actually, I thought I might take you along for protection," Elaine confessed, thinking about the way Joe had come on to her. She glanced enviously at Kit's sexy figure as she stretched in front of the mirror.

"Protection?" Kit hooted. "How can you have a mad fling with a nosy bodyguard hanging around?" She poked through the drawer, looking for a halter to go with her red shorts. "Listen, Elaine, if you're going to fling, fling. If you're not, then stay home. But you really have to decide, one way or the other."

"Well, I suppose you're right," Elaine conceded grudgingly.

She remembered the way Joe had held her as they had danced the other night. Her heart began to beat faster at the memory.

"I *know* I'm right," Kit said firmly. "Anyway, I don't have time to be your bodyguard today. Lori and Alex and I are going shopping in Lahaina." She stretched and yawned. "I intend to spend every precious cent of my year-end bonus on a Christmas present for Justin." She consulted the calendar on the desk. "After all, I'll be seeing him in only six days." She held up her hands. "Twenty-four hours times six. I wonder how many that is."

"One hundred forty-four," Elaine said promptly, pushing the covers aside.

"I've never understood how you do that," Kit retorted, envy in her voice. "I've never been any good at doing multiplication in my head, especially when you've got to carry something. I guess I just don't have the mentality for it."

"That's silly," Elaine protested. "Anybody can do multiplication." She leaned forward. "You see, all you have to do is . . ."

"Stop!" Kit squealed, putting her hands over her ears and fleeing into the bathroom. "I'm on vacation! I don't want to hear any numbers!"

With a giggle, Elaine trailed her friend and sat cross-legged on the toilet lid while Kit turned on the shower. "Listen, Kit," she persisted in teasing explanation, "all you have to . . ."

Kit burst into loud song. "I'm an old cowhand," she sang in an off-key voice, drowning out Elaine's calculations, "from the Rio Grande." It was a song the Fearless Four had done together in a Glenwood show their junior year.

". . . twenty-four," Elaine said gleefully, raising her voice above Kit's singing. "Put down four and carry two. Then you . . ."

"And my legs ain't bowed," Kit bellowed, "and my cheeks ain't . . ."

". . . times six is twelve plus two is . . ." Elaine went on, in an even louder tone of voice.

". . . tanned!" Kit screeched.

". . . one hundred forty-four." Elaine chortled. "Really, Kit. It's *so* elementary! I don't understand why you can't . . ."

"Shut up!" Alex exclaimed, leaning against the bathroom door. She was wearing a yellow stretchy headband to match her yellow shorts and T-shirt. "What are you two yelling about? I could hear you all the way down at the beach! It sounded like somebody was being murdered!"

"Somebody's about to be," Kit said darkly, reaching for the fluffy terry towel that hung on the door, "if she doesn't stop trying to tutor people in higher mathematics when they're taking a shower."

"Higher mathematics!" Elaine scoffed. She picked up the toothpaste and started to brush her teeth. "Nobody would call fourth-grade arithmetic 'higher mathematics'!"

"Well, I have a suggestion for you, Professor Gregory," Kit said loftily. "I suggest that you take your mathematics out to the beach with you and practice them on Joe." She gave a wicked snicker. "I'm sure *he* will appreciate them. Maybe he can learn to count the number of times he"—she ducked the sponge that Elaine flung at her—"flexes those muscles," she said, as she went into the bedroom to get dressed.

Elaine collapsed onto the edge of the bathtub, toothpaste foam at the corner of her mouth. "Poor Kit," she mourned. "She never did have a sense of humor when it came to arithmetic."

"So today's the day you're planning to have your fling," Alex said thoughtfully.

Elaine got up and rinsed out her mouth. "I wish you wouldn't make it sound so *calculated*," she said, her smile fading. "I mean, all I want to do is to have a little fun. I've been working like crazy at school. All I want to do is relax and forget about it. I know Joe isn't exactly my type, but . . ."

"You don't have to apologize," Alex said with a wide grin, hugging her. "For Pete's sake, Elaine, we *all* have to give in to our impulses sometime. And this *is* your vacation, after all. So go have your fling and stop worrying about it."

It was easy enough for *Alex* to tell her to stop worrying, Elaine thought, as she pulled her white cover-up over her bikini and went down the stairs to the beach. Alex never had any trouble dealing with boys, or being playful or having fun. And Kit had always had Justin, so she'd never had to worry about dates. Even if Justin weren't around, she wouldn't have to worry. The boys would always beat a path to her door.

But it seemed to Elaine that romance had always come a lot harder for her than for any of the others. Last year, she'd developed a terrible crush on Rusty Hughes, a guy she tutored in algebra. The trouble was that Rusty hadn't been able to see past her brains and her tortoiseshell glasses. Then there'd been Carl Schmidt, boy psychologist. *Their* romance—if you could call it that—had been anything but smooth sailing, even in the very beginning. Carl had hidden behind his high IQ in the same way she'd hidden behind her glasses, and the electricity had simply flickered out of their relationship.

And after that, there'd been Zack. Their relationship had always seemed charged with too *much* electricity. That had been fine for a while, but the intensity just kept getting turned up, and after a while Elaine had to admit that she wasn't ready for a long-term commitment. After all, she had three and a half years at Stanford in front of her. All she wanted *now* was a good time with somebody who didn't expect anything from her.

"Hi!" Joe was waiting for her at the foot of the stairs, and Elaine's eyes widened at the sight of him. He was wearing a pair of very brief, high-cut white trunks that showed far more of his bronzed, heavily muscled body than Elaine had seen yet.

Joe's eyes roamed over her body, and Elaine felt her face flush at the intimacy of his gaze. She clutched her cover-up around her more tightly, suddenly conscious of the skimpiness of her bikini.

"Hey, you don't need to do that," Joe said in a loud voice, grabbing her hands so that the cover-up fell open. "How come you want to go hiding such a great body?"

Great body? Elaine blushed even redder. Nobody had ever told her she had one before. Fortunately, Joe didn't give her time to think about how she was going to respond. He yanked her toward the ocean, nearly jerking her off her feet. "Come on," he commanded, "the surf's really up. Let's get out there."

With apprehension, Elaine looked out at the heavy surf, for the first time really aware that she was actually going to have to throw her body into the churning water. At first Joe had invited her to go board surfing, but when she'd said that she wasn't sure she could manage it, he'd suggested bodysurfing instead. "It's easy," he'd said. "Anybody can do it." In the heat of the moment, with his muscular arms holding her close, she'd agreed. But now she wasn't so sure.

"Listen, Joe," she said nervously, "I'm not so sure that I . . ."

"Now, don't go freakin' out on me," Joe cautioned.

Elaine tried to regain her composure. "Is it . . . is it *hard*?" she asked.

"Naw," Joe said. "It's easy." He pointed to where two boards, short versions of the surfboard, were stuck in the sand, standing straight up. "See, we'll paddle out with our bodyboards out there, past where the waves are breaking. Then all you have to do is pick a wave that looks like it'll hold up . . ."

"Hold up?"

"You know. Looks big enough to make it in close to the shore. Then you get in it and kick yourself sort of sideways in it."

"Parallel? You mean, at a right angle to the beach?" She wished that Joe would explain things better. If she had explained things to Rayne in this fashion, Rayne would have *flunked* calculus.

"Yeah. Then you just ride it, like you're a fish or a duck or something." He got a faraway look in his eyes. "Listen, don't worry. It's really fun out there, you'll see. I can show you tubing and barrel-rolling and . . ."

"What?" Elained asked in confusion.

Joe looked at her scornfully. "Honestly, Elaine, don't you know anything about this stuff?"

Elaine couldn't help smiling. For once in her life, she wasn't being called the Brain. For a change, somebody actually thought she was *dumb*! She looked up at Joe with what she hoped was a look full of implication.

"No," she said, in a voice that she had heard other girls use to boys they were interested in. "Actually, I don't know very much. About surfing, that is."

His gaze softened, and there was a new gleam in his neon-blue eyes. "Well, sure," he conceded, slipping his arm around her waist and eyeing her bikini. "Where you come from, they probably don't *have* good surf like this."

"Probably," Elaine agreed. She wasn't sure. She'd never tried surfing back in the Bay area "What's tubing?"

"Tubing is when you're inside the wave," Joe said, gesturing with his hands, "sort of like being in a tunnel. You're riding along with the crest of the wave breaking over you."

"And barrel-rolling?"

Joe grinned, flashing very white teeth. Elaine was glad to see that the two front ones were slightly crooked. It meant that he wasn't a totally perfect physical specimen.

"It's when you . . . well, you know, you roll over like a barrel, like . . ."

"Like rolling over completely?" Elaine suggested, while Joe struggled with the concept. "As in three hundred and sixty degrees?"

He flashed her a grateful look. "Yeah," he said. "But a three sixty is something else. In a three sixty, you . . ." He moved his hands to show her. "See, you do this, and then you . . ." He frowned. "Actually, it's more like a belly spin. But you've got to be careful, because you can really lose it."

"Lose it?"

"Yeah. Like wipeout, when the wave closes out under you."

"Maybe we'd better just paddle out there so I can watch you," Elaine suggested. "Maybe that way I'll get the hang of it."

"Yeah, you probably will," Joe said, grabbing her hand again. "Come on, let's go."

They swam out with their boards past the breakers, Joe's bronzed body glistening as he stroked powerfully through the waves. Elaine had noticed with a great deal of pleasure that as they went down the beach other girls were looking at them, admiring Joe's tanned, muscular body. There was a lot to admire, she thought, especially if he kept his mouth closed. She shoved that critical thought out of her mind and concentrated on swimming hard to keep up with Joe, reminding herself again that she didn't need an intellectual giant for a fling. All she needed was a body — and it looked to her as if she had picked the most beautiful one on the island.

Bodysurfing was a brand new experience for Elaine. Joe was truly good at *showing* her how to do it, even though he hadn't been very good at explaining it. There was a wonderful, bouyant feeling when the wave lifted her up and carried her along, just cresting over her head. And skidding sideways down the face of it was a little like tobogganing down a steep ski slope.

They swam and bodysurfed for nearly an hour, then made their way back to the beach, where Joe spread a towel in a secluded spot. It wasn't a very *large* towel, Elaine noticed nervously, even though he obviously intended for both of them to lie on it. She tugged at her bikini, trying to make sure that all the pieces were properly adjusted.

Joe sat down and began to dry off, and Elaine sat down beside him and toweled her hair. For a few minutes, she wondered what she was going to say, but then she decided she didn't need to worry. Joe was never at a loss for words, and she soon found herself listening to his life story. She discovered that he had dropped out of high school when he was sixteen in order to work at the hotel and give surfing lessons. His goal in life, he told her, was to win the $50,000 Men's World Cup and use it to go on a round-the-world tour of every surfing beach.

Oh, well. Elaine told herself, watching him out of the corner of her eye, *with a body like his, who cares about brains and ambition?* There were plenty of brains hanging around the library at Stanford, but she hadn't noticed any bodies like Joe's there. Tentatively, she put a hand on his bicep and he stopped in mid-sentence to face her.

"Like that, huh?" he asked, looking down proudly at his muscle.

Taken aback, Elaine stammered, "Well, uh, yes, I . . . yes, I guess I do."

"I lift weights," Joe explained. "Like at the gym, you know? Three times a week." He flexed his bicep for her approval. "Good for the old bod," he said. "Actually, you can't do too much for the old bod. After all, it's the only one you've got. Right?"

"Oh, right," Elaine agreed, trying not to laugh. "You can't do too much for the . . . for the old bod."

"But listen," Joe said earnestly, bending so close to her she could scarcely see his face, "talk about bods, I've really got this thing for yours, Elaine."

"You have?" Elaine said dreamily, pulling back a little so that she could focus her eyes on his lips. He had a full, sensuous mouth. How would it feel when he kissed her? Her insides felt warm, and her stomach did a flip. He *was* going to kiss her, wasn't he? He couldn't talk forever. Elaine moved her thigh a little closer to the curve of his.

"Yeah," Joe said huskily. "You've got a beautiful body." He reached a muscled arm around her waist and pulled himself over until he was nearly on top of her. "You turn me on, Elaine."

She closed her eyes as he brought his mouth down to hers, gently at first and then more insistently. For what seemed like forever, he kissed her passionately, his fingers buried in her hair. Then his lips moved to the curve of her throat and she felt his warm hand on her leg. For an instant Elaine stiffened, and then she forced herself to yield. *How can you have a fling if you aren't willing to let yourself go?* she asked herself, submitting to Joe's feverish kisses.

But something was wrong. Something was missing. The passion and excitement she'd expected just weren't there. Was it Joe's fault? Or hers? Was she just too responsible and serious to *have* a fling? With a determined sigh, she concentrated on the feel of Joe's firm, muscular back under her fingertips. She had wanted excitement without the complications of commitment, and that was exactly what she was getting. She might as well relax and enjoy it. Still, she thought as she pushed his hand off her thigh, she was very glad that they were on a *public* beach.

Chapter Eleven

Lahaina was one of Hawaii's most historic towns, the girls discovered when they got there. Now a quaint port town filled with dozens of little shops, in the eighteen-fifties it had been the whaling capital of the Pacific. In those days, the harbor had been jammed with hundreds of wooden vessels from all over the world. Elaine, reading the guidebook, had told them how the Hawaiian women, feeling hospitable, had swum naked out to meet the sailors—the sort of hospitality that the upright missionaries frowned on severely. Now, there was no swimming permitted in the harbor, and only a restored German whaler, a wooden square-rigged brig called the *Carthaginian II,* was tied up in the port and open to tourists as a floating museum.

"But where do we *park*?" Lori wailed, on their third trip down Front Street, which was

140

crowded with cars and pedestrians. "It's almost as bad as trying to find a place to park in Carmel." Carmel was a quaint little seaside town in California, only an hour's drive from Glenwood.

"Nothing could be as bad as parking in Carmel," Kit said. "Look! There's a space." She pointed to one sandwiched between two camper trucks. "We just have to remember to come back every couple of hours and feed the parking meter, that's all."

"I'll set the alarm on my watch," Alex volunteered. "That way we won't have to worry."

"Oh, Alex, you are so disgustingly well organized," Kit said, as they got out of the parked car. "I bet you were born with a calendar in one hand and a watch in the other."

"Yes," Lori giggled. "A stopwatch."

Kit admired Alex for always being organized and on time. She herself was incredibly scatterbrained and went about things in a haphazard way. She had always been late with assignments in school, and often she missed appointments. Once she had even slept through a final. Now that she was working and going to school, she was trying hard to keep her life in some sort of order. But even though she was more successful, she knew it was never going to be easy for her, the way it was for Alex. In fact, she thought, that was one of the things she loved about Justin. He was super-organized, just like Alex, and if they got married, she would never have to worry about things getting done on time. Justin would take care of everything.

"Where shall we start?" Lori asked. Kit and Alex were dressed in shorts and bright Hawaiian-print blouses, with their jogging shoes for comfortable walking. Lori was wearing a pair of blue-and-white seersucker pants with the cuffs rolled up, white sandals, and a cornflower-blue sleeveless blouse exactly the shade of her eyes. She looked stunning, Kit thought, feeling like a kid in her shorts and sneakers.

The girls walked down Front Street toward the old wharf. Ramshackle buildings lined the narrow street, under old weathered balconies, their railings festooned with exotic tropical vines. Most of the windows, some of them stained glass, were fitted with heavy green shutters designed to protect them from hurricanes. Strains of Hawaiian music and reggae drifted through the air, along with the vines' sweet fragrance.

"Let's start with some coconut juice," Kit suggested, as they paused in front of a street-side stand that advertised big glasses of it, ice cold. Lori refused, but Kit and Alex each got a cup, and they walked down the street, sipping as they went. They walked past the Pioneer Inn, which looked strangely familiar to Kit. She decided she must have seen it in some old South Seas movie.

"Oh, look," Alex said. "Isn't that the place Elaine was reading to us about?" She pointed toward a rambling wooden building that looked very old. It had a painted wooden sign on it that said WHALER'S MARKET PLACE, and there were tubs of tropical trees out in front. "It's recently been restored to look the way it did years ago. And inside there're all these shops. Shall we go in?"

For the next two hours, the girls wandered happily around inside the Market Place, browsing in quaint little speciality shops, looking at batik fabrics imported from the South Seas, scrimshaw made by Alaskan Eskimos, jade carvings from China, and pink-and-black coral jewelry from the reefs north of Lahaina. After they left, they walked down Front Street toward the park, enjoying the sun. Kit and Alex nibbled on cones of pineapple- and guava-flavored shaved ice, a favorite Hawaiian treat.

In the South Seas Trading Post, Kit bought a beautiful scrimshaw carving of a whaling ship, on a small inlaid ivory box, for Justin's Christmas present. She was sure he would love it. Holding the box in her hand and imagining how delighted he would be when he saw it, Kit felt a sharp pang. She really *did* miss him. It had been such a long time—it seemed like an eternity—since they had seen one another.

At the same shop, Alex bought a beautiful hand-embroidered ruby silk kimono from Japan and a pair of ivory-handled chopsticks. A few stores farther down, Lori, with giggles and blushes, bought a beautiful handmade Indonesian sarong and was given a lesson in the art of wrapping it around herself—and *keeping* it wrapped. A few minutes later, as they walked by a shop called Sam's Shirt Front, Kit's eye was caught by a lime-green T-shirt that was printed with the phrase "Just Mauied" on it. When she went into the store, she saw a blue one that announced "Happily Mauied," so she bought it too. Alex, not to be outdone, bought one with palm trees and a whale on the front that said "When God Made Maui, She Did a Whale of a Job."

"Is one of those T-shirts for Justin?" Alex asked Kit as they left the shop and walked down the street toward an old church they had decided to see.

Kit smiled self-consciously. "I don't know," she shrugged. "I guess so, if he wants one."

Lori turned to her. "You haven't said much

about what you're planning to do about getting engaged," she observed.

"I guess that's because I've been thinking about it so much," Kit confessed.

It was true. She *had* been thinking about it. She and Justin had been together for a long time now, so long that she could barely remember the string of boys she had casually dated in the era BJ, as they used to joke. Before Justin. When she thought about those times, she almost felt like shriveling up. The boys she had dated back then had made it clear they were only after one thing. Her round blue eyes, the mouth that seemed to gather itself into a permanent heart-shaped pucker, and her curvy figure. None of them ever took the time to figure out if there was more to her than what was on the outside.

But Justin Kennerly had been different. Justin had been the very first to care about what was *inside* her. With his logical, serious turn of mind, he was always thinking ahead to the future, always planning for tomorrow, or next week, or next year. That was why he had been so successful all his life, Kit knew, and that was probably why he was asking her now to get engaged. It was just like Justin to want to make plans for a future that was at least four or five years away. That kind of planning was very hard for Kit to do.

In fact, in most of the ways that really mattered, Justin was her exact opposite. The idea that somebody like that could care for her—somebody so self-confident and thoughtful and reliable—had at first seemed almost impossible. They had been together long enough to prove it wasn't impossible, but it still seemed an awfully unlikely match, and Kit was sure that if they ever broke up she would never find anyone like him again.

And *that* mattered. The image of Justin came to her—his calm gray eyes, his crooked smile, his lean, angular face. It was a face she loved. Losing Justin would almost be like losing the center of her life, or breaking the bonds that held the scattered pieces of her selves together. In a way, it would be like losing the locomotive that pulled the train. Not that she didn't have her *own* dreams for her life, dreams built around professional dance. She did. That was why she was living in New York, away from Justin, and studying at Juilliard. That was why she worked so hard at her dance—harder than any of her friends could ever guess.

"Oh, look," Alex said. Kit looked where she was pointing. They had come to the Waiola Church, one of the most beautiful buildings in the village. It was a simple, white painted church with decorative trim and gorgeous stained-glass windows that sparkled like jewels. A bridal couple was just emerging from the front doors, into a hail of rice thrown by cheering friends. The bride wore a traditional white gown and a frothy white veil, and she looked so radiantly happy that Kit's eyes grew misty and her throat hurt.

Is that what their wedding would be like if she and Justin got married? Kit thought dreamily. Would she wear a full-length white satin gown and a drifting veil? Which of her best friends—Elaine, Lori, Alex—would catch her bridal bouquet as she tossed it? She sighed happily. What a beautiful fantasy it was—but it didn't have to be a fantasy, she reminded herself. If she said yes to Justin, the fantasy would be that much closer to coming true.

"It's nearly twelve-thirty," Lori said, interrupting Kit's thoughts. "Aren't you guys hungry? Kevin told me that one of the best places to eat in Lahaina is a place called Kimo's, where the menus are inscribed on coconuts."

"Listen, before we have lunch, I'd like to go to the harbor," Alex said.

"What for?" Lori asked curiously.

"Danny's supposed to come in today, but I don't know what time. While we're here, we might as well look and see."

The harbor was full of sailboats, as well as the short, stubby fishing boats that went out early every morning to supply the stores and restaurants of Maui. There were plenty of charter boats, too, taking people out to fish, scuba, snorkel, or sightsee. The harbor was a busy place, and the docks were crowded with people carrying sailing gear, buckets of fish, coils of ropes, and cans of gasoline.

The girls' timing couldn't have been more perfect. They arrived at the harbor just in time to see a forty-foot sailing yacht tying up at the end of a nearby pier, its teak trim and chrome rails glistening against the shining hull and clean white sails. The name DOLPHIN III was printed across the stern, and under that the words LOS ANGELES.

"Danny!" Alex squealed and hurled herself toward the tall boy who had jumped off the boat and was tying it up. Kit and Lori watched as the two flung themselves into each others' arms and did a little dance out on the end of the dock.

"Just friends?" Kit said to Lori, laughing. Somehow, the greeting looked a little more affectionate than a meeting between friends.

Lori smiled. "That's what Alex said." She watched them with what looked to Kit like envy. "I've always thought they were a terrific-looking couple, even if they do look sort of mismatched."

Kit nodded, watching, too. She understood exactly what Lori meant. Danny was tall, with light brown sun-streaked hair and blue eyes, while Alex was short and tawny skinned, with straight, mahogany hair and half-Oriental features. But they had always seemed to make a good team, and Kit had never quite understood why they had broken up.

"Come on," Alex called excitedly, waving at them. "We're invited on a tour of the *Dolphin*!"

Danny hugged Kit and Lori. His blue eyes were dancing with pleasure and he was even taller and tanner than he had been the last time Kit had seen him, at graduation. He looked around.

"Where's Elaine?" he asked, slipping his arm around Alex's waist. "I thought she was with you, too."

Kit giggled, thinking of Elaine and Joe. She wondered how it was going. "Elaine is out with a guy," she said. "A surfing instructor. We met him on the beach the other day."

Danny raised an eyebrow. "Professor Elaine Gregory? Out playing with a beach bum? What's the world coming to?"

Alex laughed. "Elaine's having a *real* vacation," she said.

At that moment, they were joined by a tall,

handsome boy in white cutoffs and a navy tank-top that showed off his walnut-dark tan. His curly hair was sun streaked, Kit noticed, and he had a thick blond moustache. His eyes were a beautiful shade of green, nearly the color of a jade carving she'd seen in one of the shops this morning. There was something about him that caught her attention, but she wasn't sure what it was.

One thing was certain, though, Kit realized suddenly. *She* had caught *his* attention. He was giving her what she had come to recognize as the Look. The Look flashed a not-so-subtle message, which she had discovered about the time she grew out of her first A-cup bra. *I like what I'm looking at,* it asserted. Of course, as she had once told Elaine, there were variations on the Look. There was the Cool Look, the Hot Look, the Appraising Look, the Arrogant Look—and probably a dozen others she hadn't encountered yet.

She felt herself growing warm under the boy's direct gaze, but she found herself smiling at him anyway.

"Hi," he said, holding out his hand. "My name's Sean. Sean O'Donnell."

"I'm Kit McCoy," Kit said. Her hand tingled as he took it, and the shock seemed to travel up her arm to her shoulder.

Danny laughed. "Sorry, I'm forgetting my

manners," he apologized. "Alex, Lori, this is Sean. He's a student with me at UCLA. His dad owns the *Dolphin*."

"It's a terrific-looking boat," Kit said, gazing at the tall mast and gleaming chrome fittings.

"It sails the way it looks." Sean laughed. He moved a step closer to Kit. She could smell the crisp, lemony scent of his shaving lotion. "Dad and I usually take it out every holiday, to Mexico or up to Vancouver, or to Hawaii. But this year he couldn't go, so I asked Danny to be my first mate."

"You two sailed this big boat from Los Angeles all by yourselves?" Alex said.

"Not exactly. We had a couple of other crew members but they got off in Honolulu," Danny said. He picked up a loose line and wrapped it around a cleat, while Alex and the others watched.

"Would you girls like to come on board and have a look?" Sean offered. He was talking to all of them, but Kit thought that he was *looking* mostly at her. His green eyes drew her in, and there was an odd, bubbly giddiness in her head.

With excited laughter, the girls clambered on board. Danny and Sean demonstrated how the mainsail came down and wrapped neatly around the boom, while the jib rolled up around the forestay with the push of a button. They went below, down a steep wooden ladder and into the galley, where Sean showed them the gimbeled stove and table, which swung back and forth to accommodate the heeling of the boat under sail.

"We never have any spilled coffee," Sean said with a laugh, his teeth even and white under his moustache. Kit found herself wondering what it would be like to be kissed by somebody with a moustache. Then she berated herself. Just a few minutes ago, she'd been standing in front of a church, dreaming about the wedding she and Justin might have. And here she was wondering how it would feel to be kissed by a boy she had just met. She shook her head. What was going on with her?

"And this is the captain's stateroom," Sean was saying, leading Kit forward into the bow of the boat while the others stayed in the galley, getting soft drinks out of the tiny refrigerator. The walls of the stateroom were paneled with a rich, dark wood, and the wide bunk was covered with a velvety throw. Even the floor was carpeted. It was elegant and luxurious. Kit found herself staring at the bed. A pair of swimming trunks were thrown carelessly across the foot, and a terry robe hung on the back of the door. The door to the tiny bathroom was open, and she could see Sean's shaving things on the shelf. It was like being in his bedroom.

"Do you like it?" Sean asked Kit, with a smile.

"Oh . . . yes," Kit stammered. "It . . . it's very luxurious."

Sean looked around. "Yeah," he said casually. "The boat makes a neat bachelor's pad. When we're in port, I sometimes have parties. He grinned at her again, and Kit felt the skin on the back of her neck prickle. "Do you ever get down to Los Angeles?" he asked.

Kit's head swam. "No," she said, "not very often. I mean, I . . . I live in New York. I go to school there, at Juilliard."

"Too bad," Sean said regretfully. "I'd like to invite you out for a party some weekend." He brightened. "But at least we have a couple of days here in Maui. How about going sailing with me the day after tomorrow? We'd go tomorrow," he added, "but I heard something I don't like in the engine, and I want to get it checked out."

For a second, Kit was terribly tempted. What Justin didn't know wouldn't hurt him—and anyway, what difference did it really make? They would only be going sailing. Anyway, it was her vacation. She deserved a break from the humdrum routine of classes and work at the restaurant. She'd been turning down dates ever since she had moved to New York. It was time she had a little fun. It was on the tip of her tongue to say yes.

But immediately she felt guilty. How *could* she be thinking of getting engaged to Justin, if she was attracted by the first good-looking guy who came along? What kind of a girl *was* she, anyway?

"I'm sorry," she said. "I can't."

Sean was unperturbed. "Well, think about it," he said. As they left the stateroom, he put his hand on the back of her neck. Kit's skin burned where he touched it.

Chapter Twelve

Alex woke up with the birds, just as the sun was beginning to sift through the window blinds. She stretched and yawned, and then lay still for a few moments, thinking about the events of yesterday — and especially about the way she had felt when she'd walked down the dock and seen Danny for the first time. For a minute, she hadn't recognized him, but when he turned and she saw the familiar square jaw and broad shoulders, she had known who it was. At that moment, there had been a peculiar tightening in her chest and her heart had begun to pound, almost in the old way. But, that had been caused by the joy of seeing him after such a long time, she told herself. It didn't have anything to do with the way she felt about him now. He was just a good friend, somebody she had loved very much, once upon a time. Somebody she had left behind on the way to growing up.

Still, she couldn't get over how much Danny had changed in the few months since graduation. He was taller, his voice was deeper, and his shoulders *were* broader, even though he confessed that his schoolwork didn't give him much time for swimming and diving. His tan was darker, and his hair was a little lighter—from the Southern California sun, most likely.

But there was something else, too. Something that was different on the inside, not just on the outside. Something that made him seem more *mature*, not just older. Was it because he'd finally discovered what he really wanted to do with his life? He was studying to be an engineer, and that required discipline and a sense of purpose. Maybe Danny was just adjusting to the demands of college life. She sat up and clasped her knees to her chest. She knew from her own experience how much change took place between the last weeks of high school and the first weeks of college.

Alex sat there for a few minutes, thinking, and then she got out of bed, careful not to waken Lori, who lay curled up like a kitten, her head tucked under her arm. After she had dressed in shorts, the T-shirt she had bought yesterday, and jogging shoes, she went into the kitchen and opened the refrigerator. Yesterday she and Danny had decided that they would go hiking today at Haleakala Crater, the dormant volcano at the southern end of the island, two hours away. They had asked the others to go with them, but Lori was going somewhere with Kevin, Elaine had a date with Joe, and Kit was definitely *not* the hiking type, she had reminded them. So just the two of them were going, and Alex had volunteered to make lunch.

She smiled as she got out the peanut butter and the bananas. She wondered if anybody else in the world shared Danny's peculiar love for peanut-butter-and-banana sandwiches. Then her smile broadened, as she thought about the hundreds of times over the past few years that she had made peanut-butter-and-banana sandwiches for their outings. Trips to the beach, to the museums in San Francisco, on hiking trips to the mountains . . . .

While Alex fixed a more conventional peanut-butter-and-jelly sandwich for herself, she remembered the hiking trip that had been the beginning of the end for her and Danny. He and her foster-sister Stephanie had gotten lost in the woods and spent the whole night there together. Nothing had happened between them, but Danny had admitted that he had *wanted* something to happen, and that had shaken Alex as much as if it had. They had been drifting apart for months, and Danny had confessed that he felt that Alex didn't need him in her life.

The pain of the break-up had faded with time, but Alex knew that she would never forget his words that day. "I've always felt that I disappointed you somehow, Alex," he had said. "That you wanted me to be somebody I wasn't. Somebody more ambitious maybe. But I can't be what you want. You can't change for someone, no matter how much you love them."

At first Alex had denied what he was saying because she loved him so much. And when it was finally all over, she hadn't even wanted to see him as a friend, knowing how much it would hurt. Of course, Wes had come along after that, and his magic had helped to heal the loss of Danny's love. But it was still there, buried deep inside her. Feeling that pain again, she knew that she had made the right decision when she decided to stay away from romance.

The sound of a horn outside interrupted her thoughts, and she grabbed the backpack and ran for the door.

"Hi!" Danny reached over and opened the door of the compact car he had rented. "All ready?"

"Can we stop and get some soda?" Alex

asked, as she climbed into the car and slung the pack into the back seat. "We need some root beer."

"Absolutely," Danny said, backing out of the drive. "We can't have a hike without root beer, can we? And we can't forget the pretzels, either."

They laughed together comfortably, and she knew he was remembering the same thing she was. They were remembering the dozens of times they had stopped at the convenience store near her house, on the way somewhere, and bought root beer and pretzels.

Danny patted the dash. "Well, it's not my old truck or your Green Demon, but it'll have to do."

Alex grinned. "Poor old Green Demon," she said. "I hope Stephanie's treating it well." Alex had practically taken the engine apart once a week, trying to get it to run, and Danny had always teased her about her mechanical efforts. Thinking about the Green Demon brought back a flood of other memories, and she was silent for a moment. It was a nice feeling, she reflected, to know somebody long enough and well enough to share a past together.

After they stopped for the root beer and pretzels, they turned onto Pukalani Road.

They could see Haleakala looming ahead, over 10,000 feet high, its flanks velvety green. As they drove up the lower slopes, they passed sugar cane fields and shadowy groves of eucalyptus trees, and every now and then they could see sheer rock faces laced with silvery waterfalls. Farther up, on the middle slopes, dozens of small farms dotted the hills, where the farmers grew guavas, avocados, and lichee nuts, and horses and cattle grazed on the green meadows.

At the Haleakala turnoff, they began the twisting ascent to the crater itself. Finally, they reached the House of the Sun Observatory, more than two miles high on the rim of the crater. They parked the car at an overlook and stared out at the deep, wide crater that spread out 2,800 feet beneath them.

"Wow," Alex whispered breathlessly. "It's like being on the moon!"

The floor of the vast volcano was made of eerie heaps of cinder and ribbons of lava, softened by drifts of ash. There was a trail down the steep bluff in front of them, and grasses and small shrubs grew beside it. Farther down, the vegetation thinned out, and the ashy soil was bare. It was strange and mysterious.

Danny propped his elbows on the hood of the car, putting the binoculars to his eyes.

"Pretty spectacular," he agreed, looking off into the distance. "There are eight or nine cinder cones down there, and I read somewhere that the smallest is about the size of a sixty-story building."

"Are we going to hike down there?" Alex asked.

"Do you want to?" Danny's eyes twinkled. "What kind of shape are you in?"

Alex put her hands on her hips. "What do you mean, what kind of shape am I in?" she demanded. "I'm *always* in good shape."

Danny let his eyes rove up and down her. "Yeah, I can *see* that," he joked. "What I mean is, are you in condition for something strenuous, or do you want to just do a short hike, like down the hill and back. We could leave the lunch here and eat it when we come back."

Alex got the backpack out of the car and slipped it on. "Let's go," she said.

Danny laughed and slipped an arm around her waist. "I might have known," he said, grinning down at her. "Supergirl. Faster than a speeding . . ." He stopped himself, a brief flicker of pain in his eyes.

Alex winced. She knew what he was feeling. She wanted to say, *See, it's not worth it to care about somebody.* But she didn't say anything, and after a moment Danny dropped his arm.

"Come on, he said. "Let's get going."

The trail was marked by a faded signboard that read BUBBLE CAVE TRAIL, 6.7 MILES. As they came down the bluff, the moonscape totally enveloped them, and Alex could hardly believe that they had left the lush tropical forest only a few miles behind. It was totally quiet, except for the occasional call of a *nene*, the Hawaiian state bird. But in spite of the desolation of their surroundings, there were plenty of interesting things to look at, and Danny had brought a guidebook. So they spent time identifying the silversword plants and the fragrant *kupaoa*. Farther on, with Danny's binoculars, they spotted some feral goats, climbing nimbly along a cliff wall, their bleating barely audible in the distance.

It is odd being here with Danny, Alex thought, as she walked along behind him. He was carrying the blue backpack now, just as he had done so often on their hikes, and the familiar sight brought back a flood of memories. They were happy memories, Alex had to admit, because they'd had a lot of good times together. That was true partly because they were so different, and their differences complemented one another: her keyed-up competitiveness versus his easygoing, take-

162

it-or-leave-it style. They were exact opposites in the way they confronted life. Was that still true? Alex wondered. It seemed as if Danny had changed. Had she?

They reached Bubble Cave about noon. It wasn't a cave at all, just a large natural shelter formed when a portion of a lava bubble had collapsed. Now it was used by hikers as a rest stop, providing a welcome relief from the glare of the noonday sun.

Alex and Danny sat down and spread out their lunch.

"Terrific," Danny sighed in appreciation. "You know, I don't think I've had a peanut-butter-and-banana sandwich since the last one you fixed for me."

"That's because the cooks in your cafeteria don't know what's good for you," Alex said, putting out the pretzels and trail mix.

Danny opened the pretzels and spread them out on a rock where they both could reach them. "Do you like living in the dormitory?" he asked.

Alex shrugged. "Yeah, I guess so," she answered, unwrapping her sandwich. "But it seems like I just go there to sleep. I've got classes in the morning, and then workouts the rest of the day. It's pretty noisy on my floor, and I can't really study there, so I spend evenings in the library."

"You haven't changed much, have you, Alex," Danny said, with a brief glance at her. He took a bite of his sandwich. "It sounds as if you're still the same old go-go girl."

"I suppose I haven't changed," Alex agreed. "After all, if I'm going to make the Olympics, I've got to keep an edge."

"What do you mean, 'if'?" Danny asked with a laugh. "Since when does Alex Enomoto talk about 'ifs'?"

"Since I've met so many other girls who are every bit as good as I am—and sometimes better," Alex said. "I'm beginning to realize that sometimes there are limits to our capabilities that we don't really understand. Surprises happen that keep us from getting where we want to be. Maybe growing up is something like learning to live with those limits."

Hearing herself say the words, she was taken aback. Was that *really* how she felt? She knew it was the truth, she just had never admitted it to herself before. Noodle had known it, and that's how he was able to create such a happy life in spite of his physical limitations. Wes had known it, and that was why he had stopped racing. She filed the thought away for further reflection and turned to Danny. "How about you?" she asked, going back

164

to their subject. "You've changed. You seem . . . well, a little more intense, maybe."

Danny chuckled. "Not quite so lazy and laid-back, you mean?"

"Something like that," Alex admitted wryly. "I wouldn't have said so, but . . ."

"Yeah, well, I found out that you don't go to engineering school without having some sort of sense of direction and purpose," Danny replied. He tipped his head back and finished the last of his root beer. "I know I used to tease you about always being so gung-ho, Alex," he went on, with a hint of the old twinkle in his eye. "But part of the reason was that I used to be afraid a lot of the time."

"Afraid!" Alex gasped. That was something she would never have guessed. "Danny, that's . . . that's *weird*. What were you afraid of ?"

"Oh, I don't know. Lots of things, I guess." A salamander poked its head out from under a nearby hunk of lava, then ducked back again when it saw them. "I was afraid I couldn't keep up with you. Afraid I wasn't going to measure up to your expectations. Afraid I was going to lose you to somebody . . . well, somebody bigger and better and smarter." He looked up at her with a teasing smile. "After all, you *did* beat the heck out of me in tennis, and I really couldn't compete with you as a diver. And worst of all, you could fix your own car—you didn't even need to call me to help."

"Oh, Danny," Alex said, listening to his words tumble out. "Was it really *that* bad?"

"Oh, it was never *bad*," Danny said with a grin. "In fact, it was pretty good most of the time. But there were times when"—he gestured toward the rock where the salamander had disappeared—"I was a lot like that salamander, I guess. There were times when I just wanted to hide under a rock and stop trying to prove myself."

"I didn't know," Alex said. She cleared her throat. "You didn't tell me."

"I'm not even sure *I* knew," Danny said. He reached out and covered her fingers with his. "Maybe I didn't really understand it until later, when the pressure was finally off and I didn't have to worry anymore about keeping it all together." He looked at her for a long moment, his face shadowed in the dimness of the cave. "I . . . I didn't expect that we'd be able to talk like this," he said at last. "It's kind of a surprise to me." His fingers tightened on Alex's. "I mean, I knew that I was looking forward to seeing you, but I thought we might be . . . well, you know—kind of distant with each other. Not like this." His voice became more serious. "This feels good. It feels special."

"Yes, I know what you mean," Alex agreed, lost in her thoughts. Always before, they had disagreed on so much, and here they were, agreeing on something as fundamental and major as the way they felt about what had happened between them such a long time ago. And now that she understood how Danny had felt back then, she could understand why they had drifted apart. It made things clearer, somehow.

Alex looked down at her hand. The warmth of Danny's fingers was creeping up her arm in little tingles. He leaned toward her, and with a sharp sense of panic she recognized the look in his eyes. He was going to kiss her! This wasn't what she had wanted at all! She had just intended to keep things on a friendly basis between them—not to rekindle their old romance. Hastily, she pulled her hand away, sitting up straighter and clasping her knees against her chest with both arms.

Danny looked at her. "Is it because of Wes?" he asked. There was a raw edge to his voice. "Are you two still in love?"

Alex stared at him. "Wes? You mean . . . you don't know?"

"Know what?"

"Wes is dead," Alex said simply. "He was killed in a racetrack accident this fall."

The words fell between them like heavy rocks. There was a long silence, and finally Danny said, "Oh, Alex, I'm sorry. I didn't know." There was another silence, and then he cleared his throat. "It's been a tough year for you, hasn't it?"

The tears stung Alex's eyes and her throat felt tight. Danny was right. It *had* been a tough year. First Noodle, then Wes. And Danny had been so fantastic when Noodle died. That was when he had helped her to understand that she couldn't retreat, that she had to face the fact of her brother's death so her *own* life could go on.

But that was all in the past, she reminded herself, clasping her knees, rocking back and forth.

Danny looked at her with a tender gaze. "Are you ready to go?" he asked, gathering up the cans and empty bags.

"Yes, I guess so," Alex said. She got up and walked toward the light that spilled into the cave. There was a long silence after that, as they walked, and when they talked again, it was about Lori and Kit and Elaine and the fun they were having on Maui.

Chapter Thirteen

Lori woke up when she heard the toot of Danny's horn out in the drive and the slam of the front door behind Alex. She stretched and looked at the clock. It was only eight o'clock, and Kevin wasn't due for another hour. They had agreed to make a leisurely day of it—a drive to the other end of the island, then a walk along the tropical paths of Waianapanapa Park, and finally a swim at Pa'iloa Beach. Kevin had promised to bring lunch with him. He hadn't wanted her to worry about fixing anything for them. He would take care of everything, he had promised, when she'd agreed to spend the day with him.

"Are you awake? I thought I heard your alarm clock go off." It was Elaine, standing in the doorway. She was already dressed, in baggy khakis and a striped shirt, and her hands were thrust into her pockets.

Lori rolled over and pushed down the button on her alarm clock. "Sharing a room with Alex is like *living* in an alarm clock," she said. "I don't know how she does it."

"It's a sixth sense," Elaine explained solemnly. "Alex has something in her brain that goes tick-tock."

"I wish I had an automatic timer in my brain," Lori said, swinging her feet over the side of the bed and reaching for the lacy white robe that matched her nightgown. She stumbled into the bathroom to brush her teeth.

When she came back to the bedroom, Elaine was sitting on Lori's bed staring at the clothes in her closet. "You've brought more clothes with you on vacation than I have for a whole year," she joked, as she watched Lori pull out a pair of beige cotton pants with a double-wrap sash and ankle-tie legs. She added a bright Balinese halter top and a flowing white cover-up with big sleeves.

"What do you think of this?" she asked Elaine, holding up the outfit.

Elaine looked at her enviously. "What would you charge to be my fashion consultant?" she asked. "It would have to be on a consult-now-pay-later basis, and I couldn't give you anything until I'm out of school, but..." She threw up her hands. "It looks wonderful, that's how it looks. It looks native and romantic and . . . Where are you going?"

"To the beach, with Kevin," Lori said, absently getting out her makeup kit and going to the dressing table. She turned on the mirror light. "What about you? What are you doing today?"

"Kit and I are going to take Alex's advice and go snorkeling at the reef," she said. "But knowing Kit, it'll be at least noon before we get out of here."

"What about Joe Kendall?" Lori asked, patting on her foundation. "How was your day with him yesterday? Didn't you two go bodysurfing?"

Elaine blushed. "It went okay," she said. "At least the bodysurfing part of it. I guess I just have to get used to a few things about life."

Lori raised one eyebrow as she put on some blue eye shadow. "Like what?"

"Like making out on a public beach with somebody you don't even know," Elaine said, in a voice barely above a whisper.

"Oh," Lori said. She began to apply mascara. "Is that what you and Joe did?"

"Well, some of the time, anyway," Elaine said. "I mean, I know that it isn't a big deal, and that everybody else does it. But *I've* never done it, even with somebody I like a lot. In fact, I've never even kissed a boy I didn't think

I loved! Until yesterday, that is," she added, pulling up her knees and propping her chin on them.

Lori swiveled around to face Elaine. "Elaine, are you *sure* about this fling? I know he's good-looking and all that, but what do you find to *talk* about with him?"

"It's true, we have nothing in common," Elaine explained. "But that's just the point."

"Of what?" Lori lightly applied some blush and then stared in the mirror, surveying the job she had done.

"Of a fling," Elaine explained patiently. "I don't want to get involved. I want to have the fun of getting to know somebody without all the complications of a *relationship.* So, the best way to do that is to pick somebody cute who is *not* your type. Don't you think so?" She waited expectantly, watching Lori put on her lipstick.

"I suppose so," Lori said, unconvinced. She wiped at a smudge of lipstick on her chin and then got up and went into the bathroom.

"Well, I wasn't so sure in the beginning, either," Elaine confessed, getting off the bed and following Lori as far as the bathroom door. "But I think I'm on the right track now. All I have to do is relax and enjoy it, like everybody else." She looked up in surprise as Lori started washing her face. "What are you *do-*

ing? Didn't you just put on your makeup?"

Lori went back into the bedroom, after drying her face with a towel. "Yes," she said, "I put on my *working* face."

"You mean your modeling face?" Elaine asked."What's wrong with that?"

"I don't *want* to look like a model," Lori replied, as she brushed her hair. "I want to look like *me* for a change." She pulled on the beige pants and added the colorful halter top. "I want people to treat me like *me*, and not like somebody they just want to take a picture of."

Elaine stared at her. Then she shook her head. "If you ask me," she said, "it doesn't make any difference whether you're wearing makeup or not. You *still* look like somebody who just walked out of a magazine."

Kevin picked her up in a white Mercedes. He whistled softly when he saw her.

"Perfect," he muttered, under his breath. He looked her up and down, his eyes intent. "You're absolutely perfect. Nobody else will do for it."

"What did you say?" Lori asked. On her way down the hall she had picked up a battered wide-brimmed straw hat with a red ribbon around it, probably a relic of one of Clare Karlysle's visits to the island. Now, she slung her hat into the back of the car and got in.

Kevin shook his head. "I said *Honi Kaua wikiwiki*," he said. He picked up her hand and kissed her fingers.

"And what does that mean?" Lori asked.

Kevin's eyes sparkled. "It means "Kiss me quick," he said, and leaned forward and kissed her on the lips. As Lori blushed, he added, "I hope you brought your swimsuit."

"It's in my bag," Lori said teasingly. She still wasn't as good at flirting as some of the models she knew, but at least she wasn't as serious as she'd been back at Glenwood.

"And just to firm up the schedule," he went on, as he backed out of the drive, "I hope you've saved tomorrow for me. I thought we'd go skiing."

"I'm not sure about that," Lori said doubtfully. "I've never water-skiied before." And anyway, she thought to herself, Kevin Duvall was taking *way* too much for granted.

"Oh, I wasn't talking about waterskiing," Kevin said nonchalantly, as they pulled out onto the highway. "I was talking about snow skiing. We've got reservations on a ski trip up to Mauna Kea."

Lori stared at him. "You've got to be joking," she said. "The sun is shining and it's eighty degrees." She looked around. "The only snow here is in people's imaginations."

"Oh, yeah?" Kevin pointed to the bumper

sticker on the car in front of them. It urged THINK SNOW. "Well, how do you account for that, then?"

"I'd say that car came from California, that's what I'd say," Lori laughed.

"Well, you'd be wrong," Kevin replied. "And I'll prove it to you. Be ready at six in the morning."

"What happens at six in the morning?" Lori asked suspiciously."

"At six I pick you up," Kevin said. "At seven-thirty we're on the plane to Wiamea, on the island of Hawaii. By nine we're in a Jeep, on the way up to Mauna Kea. By ten-thirty, we're on the slopes at twelve thousand feet. There's no lift—the Jeep picks us up at the bottom and takes us back up to the top. Don't worry about getting back. We'll catch the seven PM commuter plane back to Maui and be home by eight-thirty."

"But I *can't* go skiing. I didn't bring any ski clothes," Lori protested. "Or any skis or . . ."

Kevin threw back his head and laughed merrily. "All you need is your bikini, your sunglasses, and plenty of suntan lotion. The air is thin at twelve thousand feet, and the sun's pretty powerful."

"You're not serious," Lori said incredulously.

"I certainly am," Kevin said earnestly, turning to look at her. "Will you go?"

Lori gulped. She was blushing under the force of his gaze. "I . . . I guess so," she said, in a small voice. She turned away from him and looked out the window. What had she gotten herself into when she met Kevin Duvall?

Everything they had said about this island was true, Lori thought as Kevin maneuvered his Mercedes around the curves of the coast highway. The road hugging the eastern shore of Maui was absolutely spectacular. Every twist and turn—and there were plenty of them on the seaside highway—brought an even more incredible sight. On her right, the tropical jungle shone green as an emerald under the sun. She could see clumps of wild ginger and graceful ferns, and the umbrella-shaped leaves of what Kevin said were *ape-ape* plants, two yards wide with brown blossoms hanging under the leaves like clusters of shells. On her left, the lava headlands plunged steeply down to the sea, and waterfalls and jungle pools gleamed silver in the sun. A few miles farther along, on the Keanae Peninsula, tiny thatched-roof villages clustered near the shore. Lori thought that she must be seeing old Hawaii as it had been before the white man came and filled its beaches with condos and hotels and shopping centers. The sight gave her a peaceful feeling, as if she were experiencing a vision of a world that no longer existed.

Just beyond the little plantation town of Kaeleku, Kevin turned onto a narrow gravel road. "We're going to Waianapanapa Cave," he explained. "It's one of the most famous caves in Hawaii." They parked the car and walked the short distance to the cave, which, Kevin told her as they walked along under arching palms and papaya trees, was actually a collapsed section of a lava tube filled with fresh water.

"The legend says that a cruel Hawaiian chief suspected his wife, the princess, of having an affair with another man," he said, as they stood on the headland overlooking the cave. Lori wore Clare's wide-brimmed hat to shade her eyes. "The princess and her lover hid here, but the husband found them and murdered them. Now, every April, on the anniversary of the crime, the water in the cave turns red, the color of their blood. And if you listen, you can hear the princess weeping for her murdered lover."

"How romantic." Lori sighed, looking down toward the sunken cave. She loved romantic stories, but she hated the unhappy endings that usually came with them. Why was it that romance always seemed to end tragically, she wondered. "Does the water *really* turn red?" she asked curiously.

Kevin slipped his arm around her shoulders. "Yes, it does," he said. "I've seen it."

Lori was quiet for a minute, as she thought about the legend.

"But scientists have given a rational explanation for what happens," Kevin added. "It seems that every April, schools of tiny red shrimp appear at this spot. They're so thick that the water literally turns red."

Lori wrinkled her nose. "I liked the legend better than the scientific explanation," she said. "Fairy tales can be spoiled with too much logic."

"Maybe you're right," Kevin said. He smiled down at her, and his arm tightened. "Can you hear the princess weeping?" he asked softly.

Lori listened. From somewhere close by, she heard what sounded like a low moan.

"I hear *something*," she exclaimed. The sound rose and fell eerily among the trees. "It *does* sound like somebody crying."

"I won't give you the scientific explanation of *that*." Kevin laughed. "I don't want anything to spoil it for you."

Lori shook her head and looked out to sea. "It's too beautiful here for *anything* to spoil it," she said quietly. The surf pounded the rocks just below with an almost frightening violence, but farther out the blue ocean was smooth and tranquil, stretching away to the horizon.

Kevin gently took off her hat and tipped up her face with his fingers. "*You're* beautiful, Lori," he said, tracing the line of her cheek with delicate fingers. He leaned forward, scrutinizing her face. "Even without make-up," he added, pulling back a little. With his fingers he turned her face first one way and then the other. "Don't you wear makeup? I'd swear you had it on the other night at the ho-tel. In fact, you were wearing . . ." He stopped. "You were wearing a very attractive lipstick," he said.

Lori laughed, wondering how it was that a man would notice the lipstick she was wear-ing. "I put makeup on this morning, but then I washed it off," she confessed. "I decided not to wear my working face on vacation — except maybe at night, or for a party or something."

"Your 'working' face." He laughed lightly. "Well, *I* like your face, whether it's your work-ing face or your vacation face." His voice grew husky, and he bent to kiss her, the touch of his lips feathery and gentle at first, then more insistent, his arms tightening around her so that she could hardly breathe.

With a little gasp, Lori pulled away. "Uh, isn't it time for lunch?" she asked, trying to cover her confusion. "And I thought we were going for a swim."

Kevin dropped his arms. His breathing was ragged, and his eyes were bright. "Lunch," he said. "Yes, seems to me I remember something about lunch." Grinning, he held out his hand to Lori. "Let's go back to the car and see what goodies are waiting for us," he said.

The goodies that were waiting for them in the wicker basket Kevin had brought included, to Lori's astonishment, a complete gourmet luncheon, Hawaiian-style. Kevin had even brought a tape player, and the lilting strains of Hawaiian music filled the air. The picnic basket contained little cups of cold cucumber soup, slices of quiche Florentine, dilled shrimp salad, cheesecake, and fresh pineapple spears. Kevin spread out their lunch on a sparkling linen cloth, with real china and silver, on the glistening black sands of Pa'iloa Beach. In the middle he set a little crystal vase, which he had filled with a stunning bouquet of passion fruit flowers and fuschia blossoms that he had picked along the path.

When Lori was seated at the picnic cloth, he poured her a frothy drink from a cold thermos jug.

"To us," he said smoothly, tipping his glass

against hers. "To a long and delightful relationship."

A *long* relationship? Did that mean Kevin was thinking of seeing her when they got back to New York? Lori pushed the thought out of her mind. It wasn't something she wanted to deal with just yet. Kevin had a magnetic personality and glamorous good looks, but she wasn't sure that those were the right prerequisites for a long relationship. Although she couldn't put her finger on it, there was something about Kevin that made her slightly uncomfortable.

"What is this?" she asked, taking a sip of her drink. It was thick and cold and very sweet, and it tasted luscious.

"It's a drink made from passion fruit and coconut milk," he said, serving her a slice of quiche and a helping of shrimp salad. "Speciality of the house."

Lori looked around. The tiny, deserted pocket beach lay at the head of a narrow bay that opened out to the ocean. It was gorgeous, with low, rough lava cliffs festooned with ferns and trailing vines. The surf roared noisily through the inlets and caves farther on down the shore, but where they were, the clear water lapped quietly against the black cinder sands, which had been eroded from the surrounding cliffs.

After lunch, Kevin suggested that they go swimming. "But we have to stay close to the shore," he cautioned. "The currents here are treacherous, and the bottom drops off sharply."

Lori picked up her bag and looked around. "Where can I change?" she asked.

"Why not here?" Kevin suggested. "The beach is deserted. In fact," he added with a grin, "we might just . . ."

"I don't think I'm ready for that," Lori said, hoping he wouldn't insist. She found a nearby bush big enough to provide a screen and changed into her swimsuit. She took off her pants and folded them up on the sand, thinking about the lunch Kevin had provided. It had been a wonderful lunch, she thought happily. So carefully planned, so tastefully arranged.

And then a nagging little voice somewhere at the back of her mind remarked, "Wasn't it a little *too* carefully planned?"

Maybe it had been. Kevin had certainly attended to every tiny detail, even down to the vase for the flowers. It was like something out of a fairy tale — too good to be true.

Lori pushed the niggling thought out of her mind. It *was* like something out of a fairy tale. The beach, the lunch, Kevin's attentiveness, the ski trip he had planned for tomorrow.

Why should she spoil a fairy tale with suspicions? *You're living the kind of life every girl dreams of. Stop asking questions and enjoy it,* Lori told herself.

Kevin looked at her admiringly when she came out from behind the bush in her new blue bikini. He had changed, too, apparently without the benefit of a bush. He gave her that same scrutinizing look that she had seen that morning. Kevin's look gave her the same feeling she had had when she was being looked over for a new job. It was as though she were being mentally weighed and measured.

"You're perfect for it," he said. "Just exactly what I had in mind."

Perfect for what? was the question on Lori's lips, but Kevin didn't give her time to ask. With a chuckle, he picked her up in his arms, ran into the ocean, and dumped her in. Squealing, Lori grabbed his shoulders and pulled him in with her. They tumbled over, laughing and playing in the surf, until they were exhausted. Then Kevin spread out towels on the beach and they lay on their stomachs, toasting in the sun and listening to more Hawaiian music.

After a while, Kevin rolled over onto his side and looked at her. "You know, you're beautiful even with your hair wet," he said. "It makes the contours of your face stand out."

He touched his finger to her eyebrow, drawing a tender line down to her cheek, and then to the corner of her mouth. "Such wonderful lips," he murmured, gazing at her mouth.

As Kevin's arms came around her and his lips came down on hers, Lori thought again about how perfect everything had been today. For once, she realized gratefully, the little voice wasn't nagging her about things being *too* perfect. And when Kevin's kiss deepened, she relaxed into his arms. Why should she resist?

Chapter Fourteen

"It was the most incredible wipeout of the year," Joe was saying. He was lying facedown next to Elaine on the towel, his surfboard stuck in the sand beside them. Elaine had been watching Joe ride the waves that afternoon, although there hadn't been much action. The sea was flat and calm and little tendrils of gray mist were beginning to curl over the horizon. Finally, Joe had abandoned his efforts to get a good ride, and for the last hour, he had been telling Elaine about some of the more exciting moments in recent surfing competitions. Elaine was having a hard time staying awake.

"Along came this huge wave, a real monster, an eight-pointer, and I got up on it. I locked into the groove, and the wave began to bend into the point. But when I spun down to the lift, I took off in the hook and got disconnected from the face of it. That's when I flipped."

"How interesting," Elaine murmured. This description was a rundown on Joe's performance in the Pro Class Trials at Waimea, if she remembered right. She sat up groggily and reached for the suntan lotion.

"You haven't lived until you've surfed Waimea, baby," Joe said, rolling over on his back and shading his eyes so he could look at Elaine. "I'm going over right after Christmas. Wanna come with me?"

Elaine poured some lotion into the palm of her hand. A few yards down the beach, two bikini-clad high-school girls ogled Joe and watched Elaine with undisguised jealousy. Their envy made Elaine feel better than she had in the past hour and woke her up a bit.

"Sorry, Joe," she said. "I'd love to go, but I've got to get back to California."

"Oh, too bad. But it'll be fun anyway," Joe said. "And after that, there's the Makaha Championships, on Oahu," he added. His voice warmed and he sat up. "Now, *that's* a fun competition. There'll be a bunch of my old buddies hangin' out there, and lots of girls." He rolled his eyes. "Man, the girls on Oahu are somethin' else.

Elaine turned to him. "Would you like some lotion on your back, Joe?" she asked sweetly.

"Sure," he answered, his eyes roaming over her body. He took hold of her wrist and pulled her down gently on his chest, then placed a hand on the back of her head, bringing her lips down to his.

". . .and then the Jeep met us at the bottom of the five-mile run and took us back up again," Lori said, giving the electric popcorn popper a vigorous shake. She had just gotten back from her ski trip to Mauna Kea with Kevin. "The snow was really dry. A good fresh powder, but not very deep. And the view was incredible once the clouds cleared. Simply stunning." She sighed. "Kevin could point out every single important landmark. He's as good as a tour guide—and a lot more fun."

"Did you actually wear your bikini?" Elaine asked incredulously. She took the butter out of the refrigerator and began to heat it up on the stove. She winced a little. Even though she'd been slathering suntan lotion all over herself, she'd managed to get burned. Sunburn in December! In spite of the fact that she lived in "sunny California," winter was the foggy and rainy season. Christmas had never been like this back home.

At the thought of it, Elaine felt slightly homesick. This was the first Christmas she hadn't spent with her family. Her twin sisters,

Carla and Chrissie, were nine now, and just on the verge of giving up believing in Santa Claus. This might be the last year they would wear that special sparkle in their eyes as they fixed the plate of Christmas cookies and the glass of eggnog they always left for Santa. Her sister Andrea, at fifteen, had given up on Santa a long time ago, but the two of them still had their own special tradition: putting the silver star on top of the ten-foot blue spruce that brushed the high ceiling of the Gregory living room while the song "Silver Bells" played on the record-player.

Lori shook her head at Elaine's question. "No, I didn't wear a bikini," she said. "I wore shorts and a T-shirt. I was afraid I might get too much sun, at that high altitude. But there were some other girls up there with bathing suits on. They looked like lobsters at the end of the day." The popcorn stopped popping and she dumped most of it out into a large bowl on the counter. The rest she put into another bowl and set it aside. They were planning to string some to decorate the Christmas tree that Alex and Elaine were out buying. "How did your day go?" she asked. "Did you have fun?"

"Oh, loads," Elaine said drily. She poured the melted butter carefully over the popcorn. "If you don't count the wipeouts and the unmakable waves, all reported on a blow-by-blow basis."

Lori turned to stare. "Don't tell me," she said. "Joe Kendall's turning you into a beach bum. Worse than that—a *surfer* beach bum."

"Actually, a grommet," Elaine said with satisfaction, looking in the cupboard for the salt-shaker. "At least, that's what they call them here. Don't ask me why."

"Are you going out with him again?" Lori asked. She leaned against the counter and watched Elaine.

"Yes," Elaine answered, opening another cupboard. "He asked me to spend Christmas Eve with him at his apartment."

"His apartment?" Lori looked surprised. "Are you going to go?"

Elaine nodded. She paused, looking around her. "Have you seen the salt?"

"It's probably out beside the hot tub."

"The hot tub?" Elaine shook her head. "What's it doing there?"

"Kit ate her lunch out there this afternoon, during a long soak."

"Oh." Elaine went to get the salt and came back. "What time are they getting back with the Christmas tree? It's after eight now."

Lori consulted her watch. "That depends. How long does it take to find a Christmas tree on the day before Christmas Eve in Hawaii?"

"Maybe until the Fourth of July?" Elaine said. "*Are* there any Christmas trees in Hawaii?"

"The answer to that is no," Kit said, coming into the kitchen. "A definite n-o. I mean, there have got to be some somewhere, but not in any of the places *we* looked. And we had the feeling that half the island of Maui is driving around today, looking for the Christmas trees that the *other* half bought yesterday. That's what we get for not planning ahead."

"Oh," Lori wailed. "That's awful! What will we do?"

"Too bad," Elaine said, feeling a sharp pang of disappointment. "It's not going to seem like Christmas without a tree."

"Do not despair," Kit replied dramatically. "All is well! You don't think that the ingenious and enormously talented Christmas elves named Alex and Kit would let you down, do you?" She made a grand flourish, gesturing toward the door. "Oh Tannenbaum, oh Tannenbaum," she crooned, singing the familiar Christmas melody in an off-key soprano.

Elaine and Lori stared at the door. Nothing happened. "Oh Tannenbaum, oh Tannenbaum," Kit sang louder. "Oh, Alex, where *are* you?"

Suddenly the door opened and Alex came in. "Sorry," she said, giggling wildly. "I was laughing so hard I missed my cue." Her face was half-hidden by the large potted hibiscus bush she carried in front of her, loaded with bright red blossoms. Fastened to her forehead with tape was a majestic tinfoil star. A string of miniature Christmas-tree lights was draped around her neck.

Elaine and Lori stared speechless at Alex and the plant for a moment, and then burst into laughter. "Oh Hibiscus Bush, oh Hibiscus Bush," they all sang. "How lovely are thy blossoms!"

"I don't believe this!" Elaine said after a few minutes. Her sides hurt from laughing so hard. "A hibiscus bush for a Christmas tree! The next thing you know, you'll be telling us that you couldn't buy any eggnog to go with our buttered popcorn."

"How'd you guess?" Kit asked.

"No eggnog!" Lori exclaimed. "How can we trim the tree—the bush, I mean—without any eggnog?"

"Would you believe fruit-nog?" Alex asked. She put the bush down on the counter and produced a carton of fruit punch. "It's a mixture of passion fruit, pineapple juice, and coconut milk," she added. "It's good. Kit and I sampled it."

Alex and Kit put the hibiscus bush on a little table in front of the window in the living room and draped it with the miniature tree lights. Lori found two needles and some thread, and she and Elaine sat down to string the popcorn. They munched buttered popcorn and sipped cups of fruit-nog while the radio played Hawaiian versions of Christmas carols, complete with ukelele and steel guitar.

Lori repeated the story of her ski trip for Alex and Kit. When she was finished, she held up a long string of popcorn. "Do you think we have enough?"

Alex laughed. "That poor bush will probably be weighted down with popcorn," she said, draping Lori's string across the lower branches. She took Elaine's string and added it, as well.

Kit came into the living room, brandishing a magazine and a pair of manicure scissors. "I've got a great idea," she said. "We can cut out some Christmas pictures and hang them, too. Here's one that would be terrific. We'll let Elaine do this one." She held up a picture of a Santa Claus on a surfboard.

"Oh, no," Elaine said, putting her hands over her eyes and ducking, as if to ward off a blow. "Not another surfboard!"

"What's the matter, Elaine?" Kit teased. "Got the surfboard blues?"

"Elaine looks as if she's been bitten by the

surfboard bug," Alex volunteered.

"Or bitten by the surfboard *bum*," Kit joked.

Elaine's face burned. "Okay, you guys," she said defensively. "Enough's enough." Why couldn't they leave her alone? She was old enough to know what she wanted to do.

"Listen, Elaine." Lori's voice had a serious tone. "I really think you ought to reconsider spending Christmas Eve at Joe's. You don't really know him very well."

"At his *apartment*?" Alex asked, turning wide-eyed to Elaine. "Are you really going to do that?"

Elaine shrugged. "What's so bad about that? You can't get wet if you don't get into the water, you know."

"If getting wet is all you want," Lori said reasonably, "why don't you just stay here and spend the evening in the hot tub?" She ducked the handful of popcorn that Elaine tossed at her.

"What are *you* doing on Christmas Eve?" Elaine asked Alex, trying to change the subject.

Alex blushed a little. "I . . . I'm going sailing with Danny and Sean," she said. She looked around. "Who wants to go with us?"

"Not me," Elaine said. Defiantly, she got up to hang the surf-boarding Santa on the hibiscus bush, right under the tinfoil star that Alex had put on the very top. It didn't matter what the others said. She was tired of doing the predictable thing, of thinking through every alternative before she acted. Even more, she was tired of worrying about other people's opinions. For once in her life, she thought, she was just going to let her hair down and have a blast.

"Well, how about you, Lori?" Alex asked. "Want to go sailing?"

"Not me either, I'm afraid," Lori said. "I promised Kevin I would . . ."

"Where are you off to *this* time?" Elaine asked. "No, wait, don't tell us," she commanded. "Let us guess. You're going to see the Fiji Islands by helicopter."

"No," Alex chimed in, a wicked grin on her face. "They're going to England to celebrate Christmas with the Royal Family. Turns out that Kevin's mother was an illegitimate daughter of . . ."

"No, that's not it at all," Kit interrupted. "Kevin has rented a luxury condo at the North Pole, and he's going to pick Lori up with a team of eight lively reindeer, at 6 PM sharp."

Alex and Elaine applauded Kit's wit, and after a minute, even Lori joined in, although her face was flaming.

"Have you checked tomorrow's weather

forecast?" Lori asked Alex. "I heard today on the radio that they're expecting a storm sometime."

"There's something happening out there, that's for sure," Elaine added. "The surf was a lot flatter this afternoon, and there were some funny-looking clouds just over the horizon."

"Oh, I'm sure that Danny and Sean wouldn't take the boat out if there was any problem," Alex said. She turned to Kit. "What about you, Kit? Do you want to go sailing with Danny and me on Sean's boat?" Her grin came back, even more wickedly. "Remember Sean? The tall, blond guy with curly hair and . . ."

Kit nodded sheepishly. "I remember," she said. She hesitated. "How long are you going to be gone? I want to be sure to call Justin tomorrow night."

Alex shrugged. "Oh, I imagine we'll be back before dark. We're planning to leave around noon."

"Well, okay," Kit said, "if you insist."

"I'm not insisting," Alex said. "I mean, you're free to stay home, if you want. I'm just inviting."

"I *said* I would," Kit replied quickly. "And it's got absolutely nothing to do with Sean. Absolutely nothing."

Elaine stared at Kit. Her response to Alex,

she thought, was just a little *too* insistent. Was she interested in Danny's friend?

"You didn't have to say that," Alex said, staring at Kit. "I believe you."

"Well, good," Kit said. She picked up the pitcher. "Who wants more fruit-nog?"

"I've got an idea," Elaine said, with a glance at Kit. "Let's all take our fruit-nog and pop-corn and get in the hot tub."

There was a unanimous chorus of approval. Then Lori said, "Oh, I forgot. I left my swimsuit in Kevin's car."

"We don't need swimsuits," Alex said. "There's nobody here but us." She got up and headed for the deck, pulling off her T-shirt. She was followed by the others.

"This reminds me of the time we went skin-ny-dipping in Lori's sprinkler last year," Alex said, sliding into the warm water of the wood-en hot tub, next to Elaine. The bubbler was sending up a constant stream of fast-moving bubbles. "Except that you and Lori kept your underwear on *that* time."

Elaine laughed self-consciously. "It re-minds *me* of the time Brian Fitzgerald invited me to his place for dinner and we wound up in his hot tub. Remember, I lost my contact, and when we finally found it, Brian decided it was time to take me home."

She tilted her head back against the edge of

the tub and looked up at the brilliant stars twinkling in the Southern Pacific sky. Above her, a palm tree swayed gently with the ocean breeze and the scent of Hawaiian honeysuckle hung heavy in the soft air.

"Isn't it beautiful?" Lori asked softly. "It's hard to believe that it's Christmas. Back in New York, there's probably six inches of snow on the ground."

"And at Northwestern, the streets are jammed with traffic and the wind's blowing a blizzard," Alex added.

Elaine looked around. "Where's Kit?" she asked.

Suddenly, they heard the tape player switch on and the rhythmic sounds of the traditional Hawaiian *hula* filled the air. Kit came swaying out of the shadows, wearing a *pili* grass skirt down to her ankles and a heavy lei of flowers and leaves around her neck. She was barefoot.

Lori clapped her hands. "A *hula*!" she exclaimed. "Kit's going to dance a *hula* for us!"

"Where in the world did you learn that?" Alex asked in amazement, as Kit's undulating hips described a kind of figure eight, while her hands moved gracefully at her sides.

Kit giggled, momentarily losing her concentration. "On television," she said. "There was a program on this afternoon, teaching the *hula*, and I couldn't resist."

"This makes it a truly Hawaiian Christmas," Elaine said with a sigh, watching Kit's fluid movements, accompanied by the soft strains of traditional Hawaiian instruments. "The best Christmas ever."

"And it's not even over yet," Alex said.

"I bet it will just keep getting better," Elaine said. She leaned back, letting the bubbles caress her skin. So far it had been a wonderful Christmas. She thought of Joe and Christmas Eve and decided the best was yet to come.

Chapter Fifteen

It was a perfect day for sailing, Kit thought as she and Alex, wearing shorts over their swimsuits, made their way down the dock in the Lahanai harbor, toward the pier where the *Dolphin* was moored. The sky was blue, except for the persistent haze that hung just above the horizon, and the breeze was balmy —just the kind of soft breeze they needed for a leisurely sail. The docks were less crowded today. Obviously, not too many people wanted to go sailing on Christmas Eve.

"Hi! Welcome aboard!"

Kit looked up. Sean O'Donnell was standing in the little skiff that hung off the stern of the boat, unhooking something from the end of the boom. At least Kit thought it was the boom. She remembered a few sailing terms from years ago, before the divorce, when her father had owned a sailboat, much smaller than the *Dolphin.* He had taught her some of the basics of sailing, and even though most of the time she was really a klutz on the boat, she had tried hard to please him with her knowledge. And some of it still stuck. Maybe, she thought with anticipation, that knowledge would come in handy today.

"Hi," Kit said, waving at Sean.

"Where's Danny?" Alex asked, climbing over the rail and jumping lightly onto the teak deck.

"Down below," Sean said. "He's checking the weather with the Coast Guard."

"Is there a storm coming up?" Kit asked, as Alex disappeared down the steps into the cabin. She looked up at Sean. He was wearing a pair of white shorts and a black T-shirt that had *Dolphin II* printed on it. "One of my friends said last night that . . ."

"Oh, we may get a little blow late this afternoon, but it won't amount to much," Sean said. "Nothing to worry about." He jumped down from the skiff, his jade-green eyes resting approvingly on Kit. "I'm glad you decided to come," he said, reaching over to coil up a line. "We're going to have a great time. Have you ever sailed before?"

"My father owned a boat on San Francisco Bay," Kit said, a little tentatively. "We used to go . . ."

"Oh, then you know all about it," Sean replied confidently, before she could finish. "We won't have to worry about you."

Kit wanted to tell him that her sailing experience with her father had been a long time ago, but he didn't seem to be interested. Anyway, it probably didn't matter. With Danny on board to crew, she wouldn't have to do anything.

Danny came up from down below. "How does it look?" Sean asked.

"As you said," Danny replied. "Some weather coming up late today. But all clear until then."

"Good," Sean said, a satisfied grin on his face. He went to the wheel, a big teak-and-brass affair close to the stern. "Then what say we get started?"

Danny cast off while Sean, standing at the wheel, started the boat's inboard engine. It clicked a couple of times before it caught hold, and Sean scowled, but then it cleared and ran smoothly. Listening to it, Sean still didn't seem satisfied.

"I thought I told that guy to take care of whatever was wrong with this ignition," he said irritably.

"You did," Danny replied. "Didn't he fix it right?"

Sean shrugged. "Doesn't sound great to me. I'm going to have a little talk with him tomorrow. I don't care if it *is* Christmas Day." He motioned to Kit. "Why don't you cast us off at the stern?"

Kit looked around wildly. Cast off? Oh, yes. There were lines looped around cleats on the boat, where the boat was moored to the dock. She tossed them loose and pushed the stern off hard, while Danny went forward and did the same thing at the bow. They were off!

Once outside the Lahanai breakwater, Danny cranked up the mainsail and unfurled the jib while Sean handled the wheel. After the sails were up and filled with wind and the boat was heeled over, Sean cut the engine. There was a sudden silence, broken only by the sound of the wind in the sails, the cry of an occasional gull overhead, and the *shush-shush* of the water lapping gently at the hull.

"Oh, it's beautiful," Kit said from her seat near Sean, stretching her legs and leaning back to let her hair blow free. She looked toward the bow. Alex was sitting with her back to the mast, talking to Danny, who was leaning out, hanging onto a sidestay and looking up at the top of the mast. Around her, the teak and brass gleamed, and the entire boat was immaculate. "What a wonderful boat!"

"Yeah, it is, isn't it," Sean said, with a note of pride in his voice. He patted the wheel lovingly. "She's a real beauty."

"It must be hard to sail such a big boat," Kit observed. Sean stood with his feet wide apart, balancing against the heeling of the boat, and she admired the easy, graceful way he responded to the boat's movements.

"Oh, it's not hard if you know what you're doing," Sean said. He pushed his blond hair out of his eyes and leaned over to adjust the mainsail. "Of course, you have to be able to navigate, and you have to know what your boat will do in a storm, stuff like that." He smiled at her. "But you know how it is, since you're a sailor, too."

"Yes, but . . ." Kit began. Now was a good time to tell him that she really wasn't a sailor. But Sean's attention was fixed on the compass, and she didn't finish her sentence.

They sailed northward along the coast for several hours, tacking in and out against the breeze that blew stiffly from the northwest, over the port bow. They were two or three miles out from the shore, but Kit could peer out under the sail on the starboard side of the boat and see a long line of white sand beaches, broken intermittently by jagged sea cliffs or the emerald-green of the tropical jungle spilling down to the sea. The coast looked deserted, and there wasn't a sign of the condos and hotels that lined the beaches around Kaanapali. On the port side, the blue ocean was wide and free, and only occasionally did she glimpse a freighter steaming steadily along the horizon, leaving a trail of smoke that merged with the darker clouds behind it.

Kit took a deep breath and relaxed. She loved the feeling of freedom that surrounded her out here on the ocean, the sense that anything was possible. She wanted to tell Sean how she was feeling, but he was intent on the wheel and the sails—and anyway, it seemed like too personal a thing to say to him. She sighed. If Justin were here, *he* would understand. That was one of the things she loved most about Justin. He seemed to understand whatever she was thinking, without her saying a word.

At the thought of Justin, she felt a little pang of guilt. Would he mind her going sailing with Sean? But she wasn't really with Sean. She was with Alex, in spite of the fact that she hadn't spoken to Alex since they left the dock. She sneaked a glance at Sean. Curls of blond hair stuck to his forehead, and his muscled body gleamed golden in the sunlight. He certainly was good-looking.

After a while, Sean went below to check the chart, leaving Kit to steer. When he came up, he eased the jib and the main a little and they fell off to starboard, toward the shore, where a natural harbor had been created between two jutting headlands. A golden beach shone in the sun, a tangle of palm trees and ferns behind it.

Sean told Danny to slack off the sails, and the boat drifted almost to a stop, not very far from a small, rugged island that jutted out of the bay. Kit looked at the clear blue water of the bay, set like a sapphire in a half ring of dark rocks and golden beach. She would have liked to explore the beach, but they were too far out even to row to it. "Couldn't we take the *Dolphin* in a little closer to the beach?" Kit asked.

Sean laughed as Danny dropped the anchor off the stern of the boat. "Certainly not," he said. "This boat draws fourteen feet, and I never take it in close to shore, even if the chart says we've got sixty feet below us. Charts are wrong all the time. I'd rather be on the safe side than risk running aground or jamming a hole in the hull."

"Oh, I understand," Kit said, swallowing her disappointment. She watched as Danny lowered the sails. The boat swung lazily around, rocking with the ocean's gentle swell.

"Anyway, we're not going to run out of things to do," Sean told her. He looked at her with a gleam in his eye. "We can go swimming."

Alex came back to the stern of the boat and sat down beside Kit. She looked relaxed and happy, and Kit wondered if Danny had anything to do with it. "Is that island on your chart?" Alex asked, gesturing toward the rocky, forbidding island that dominated the bay.

"Yeah, it's called Kanaha," Sean told her. "There's supposed to be an old burial cave up on the top somewhere, from back in the days when the natives used to paddle their canoes out there to hold funerals and worship their gods. During World War II it was a munitions dump. Now it's a bird sanctuary."

"Can people go onto the island?" she asked.

Sean shrugged. "Yeah, I guess so," he said. "I don't know why you'd want to, though. You can see everything there is to see from here." He handed her a pair of high-powered binoculars.

Alex took the binoculars and began to study the jagged black rock. Suddenly she turned to Danny. "Could we take the skiff and row over to Kanaha? We don't have to stay very long. But there are some interesting-looking nests near the top that I would love to climb up and look at."

Danny looked questioningly at Sean. "Sure," Sean said. "I don't see why not."

Alex turned to Kit. "Would you like to go along?"

Kit searched Alex's face for a clue. Was it just a polite invitation? Did Alex want to be alone with Danny? She hesitated. Was she afraid of being left alone with Sean?

"No, I think I'll stay here," she said finally. "You and Danny go. You can tell me all about it when you get back."

Sean grinned. "Yeah, that's right. You can tell us about it when you get back. Kit and I won't have any trouble amusing ourselves."

Kit ducked her head, hoping that Sean couldn't see that she was blushing. She had caught his eyes on her several times in the last few minutes, and she was beginning to feel uncomfortable.

But the minute that thought occurred to her, she began to scold herself. What's the matter? Is Sean O'Donnell so sexy and attractive that you're afraid you might lose your sense of responsibility and make a pass at him? Or are you afraid that he might start coming on to you and you won't be able to resist him? Where's your faith in yourself, Kit McCoy? Can't you trust yourself to be true to Justin? She didn't know the answers.

Alex and Danny untied the skiff and lowered it into the water. They had all agreed to wait and have lunch after Danny and Alex got back from exploring the island, but Alex and Kit spent a few minutes in the galley, searching for something in which to carry some drinking water.

"Don't you have a canteen?" Kit asked Sean, poking her head up through the hatchway.

"It got lost overboard a couple of weeks ago," Sean said. He looked at his watch. "If you guys are going to go, you'd better get started."

"Oh, I guess it doesn't matter," Alex said, giving up on the canteen. "We won't be gone that long." Danny dropped a rope ladder down into the skiff, and she followed him into the boat. When they both were seated, they rowed off in the direction of the island.

After they had gone, Kit stripped down to her swimsuit and dove into the blue-green water. Sean jumped in after her, and together they swam, diving and playing like porpoises in the warm water, until they were exhausted. Then Kit climbed the rope ladder back up to the deck and toweled herself off. She fluffed out her curls with her fingers and stretched out on the deck to dry off. The sun was warm on her shoulders and she was about to doze off when Sean sat down beside her, his lean, tanned body disturbingly close.

"I suppose people tell you that you look like Goldie Hawn," he said, "with all those blond curls."

"Oh, sometimes," Kit said, shifting uncomfortably.

With a hint of laughter in his green eyes, Sean produced a tube of lotion. "How about if I do your back?"

Kit hesitated. Her first instinct was to say no. How would she feel if Justin were rubbing suntan lotion on some pretty girl's back at this very moment? But after all, it *was* only suntan lotion and Sean was probably only being nice. But as she felt the firm touch of his strong fingers stroking her back, she felt an undeniable twinge of guilt—and the guilt kept her from enjoying what might otherwise have been a very enjoyable experience.

After a few minutes, Kit began to doze again, lulled by the warm sun and the gentle rocking of the boat. Once she thought she felt Sean's lips against her bare back, where his hand had been a few minutes before, but she only sighed and stirred a little, too sleepy to respond.

Dimly, Kit began to suspect that Lori had propped their freezer door open and put a fan inside so that the cold air swooshed across the kitchen. But there was something wrong with the kitchen itself. It seemed as though the room were floating in a giant bathtub, It bobbed violently up and down until she felt seasick. She forced her eyes open—and realized that she had been dreaming. She was lying on the deck of the *Dolphin*, and the boat was wallowing from side to side in the three-foot seas that had sprung up from nowhere, churned by the suddenly cold wind. The sky was leaden-gray and ominous-looking, and a threatening squall-line marched along the ocean only a few miles outside the bay.

Kit scrambled to her feet, fear clutching her stomach. Where was Sean? But more importantly, where were Danny and Alex? She clambered toward the stern of the boat, holding on to the rail as the deck lifted and plunged under her bare feet. The skiff was still out! They weren't back yet!

The fear rose out of her stomach and into her throat. "Sean?" she shouted, panic-stricken. "Sean?"

"Yeah?" A sleepy voice drifted up from down below. "What's the problem? What's going on?"

Kit almost slid down the hatchway ladder in her terror. Sean had been asleep, sprawled on the bunk in the captain's stateroom. He sat up now and rubbed his eyes.

"There's a storm!" Kit exclaimed. "A bad storm! And Alex and Danny aren't back yet."

Sean grabbed for his deck shoes, then looked up at her, bleary-eyed. "What time is it?"

Kit glanced at her watch. "It's nearly four," she said.

Sean ran through the galley and took the ladder rungs two at a time, Kit right behind him. "Looks bad," he said, squinting at the squall line. "Could be some seventy-mile-an-hour winds in those squalls. And they're coming this way. Looks like that storm was moving a lot faster than the weather report showed." He ran toward the stern. "We're leaving," he shouted. "Get the jib." He began to hoist the anchor, putting his shoulder into it as the boat pitched and yawed under his feet. "What rotten luck," he muttered, heaving against the anchor. "My dad'll kill me if anything happens to this boat."

"But we can't leave!" Kit shouted into the rising wind. She was shivering so hard that her teeth rattled in her head. "We've got to wait for Danny and Alex! We can't leave without them!"

Sean ignored her as he continued to heave on the anchor line. "It's fast on something," he said furiously. "Probably wedged into coral or something." Suddenly he grabbed a knife from his belt and slashed the nylon line. It fell limp.

"Listen to me, Sean," Kit screamed. She wanted to pound his bare back with her hands. "We've got to wait for them."

"You listen, Kit," Sean growled, "that little dinghy will never make it out to the *Dolphin* in these seas. Danny knows better than to try. He'll stay on the island until this blows over." He turned the ignition key. It clicked twice and then went dead. He moaned.

Kit looked at him in horror. "What's wrong?" she asked in a whisper.

Sean stared at her, his face as white as the mainsail. "The ignition's out, that's what's wrong," he exploded, pounding the console with his fist. "We haven't got a motor. We're going to have to *sail* back to Lahania."

Kit went over and put her hand on the wheel. "Well, if we can't wait for Danny and Alex," she insisted, "we've got to sail over to the island and pick them up."

Sean turned on her savagely. "That's really crazy," he shouted. "We can't run the risk of running the *Dolphin* onto those rocks. It would take a really expert sailor to get a boat this size in close enough to that island to do anybody any good—and I'm no expert." He pushed her hand away from the wheel. "I'll get the main up. You handle the jib." He clambered up on top of the cabin and grabbed the boom, which was swinging wildly over Kit's head.

"But what about Alex and Danny?" Kit pleaded.

"They'll be safe where they are," he said, beginning to crank up the mainsail. "They might get a little wet and cold, that's all. Once we're underway, we'll radio the Coast Guard to send a boat after them."

Kit stared at him. "But that could take hours!" she wailed, her voice sounding small against the rising wind. She wrapped her arms around her to keep warm. "And they don't have any food or water or warm clothes. They could die of exposure!"

"I tell you, Kit, we haven't got a choice," Sean said, both hands full of line. "We don't have an anchor, so we can't stay in the bay. We'd be blown up against the beach. We've got to get out into the ocean, no matter how hard it's blowing out there." He gestured with his head. "Now go forward and unfurl that jib. And get a life jacket on," he added, as he climbed down and grabbed for the wheel.

Kit pulled an orange life jacket out of the locker at the stern of the boat, but just as she was about to put it on, a huge wave came over the stern, nearly washing her away. The life jacket was ripped out of her hands and hurled overboard in a maelstrom of white water.

"Be careful, Kit," Sean yelled at her. "That could've been you! Get another jacket out, and take care of the jib."

Shaking uncontrollably, Kit found another life jacket in the locker. Her fingers were stiff with cold as she struggled with its fastenings. Her bare feet felt numb, too, and she stumbled as she made her way forward, trying to balance against the pitching boat. Sean wanted her to unfurl the jib. Which of the half-dozen lines twisted in front of her controlled it? She tugged at one of them but the sail didn't budge. A wave crashed over the bowsprit, drenching her with icy water. She could feel her lips turning blue with cold.

"Come on, Kit. Get the jib!" Sean yelled from the stern, where he was fighting the wheel. He'd raised the mainsail only part of the way. "We've got to keep the main reefed down tight so that the boat doesn't get overpowered, and the only thing we've got to steer with is the jib. Can't you get it up?" His voice rose in a scream.

It seemed to take hours, but Kit finally managed to find the jib halyard and free the jib. She cleated the line along the rail on the leeward side and crawled back to the stern on all fours, clutching at the rail. The sky was almost as dark as night, and the boat pounded against the waves with a dull thud as they beat toward the open sea. The *Dolphin* seemed to Kit to be heeled over at an impossibly steep angle, and she clung to the rail on the high side of the boat, bracing herself with her feet to keep from sliding down under the rail and into the churning white water. Each time the boat hit a wave, it shuddered convulsively, and Kit could hear the sound of crashing glassware down below.

"These seas will be running six feet before we can get out into clear water," Sean muttered, under his breath. He eased off the jib, and the boat came up a little. They were practically flying along now, leaving the little bay behind rapidly. Kit stared at Sean, at the hard line of his jaw, his shoulders braced against the pull of the wheel. She felt a fierce hatred flaming inside her. He was the captain. The people on his boat were *his* responsibility! He should have stayed awake and watched the weather! He should have been willing to risk losing the *Dolphin* to save the lives of his crew.

Kit looked back at the island. It looked jagged and forbidding, even at this distance. There wasn't a tree or a shelter on it anywhere. Where were Alex and Danny? Were they safe? Or were they out in the skiff, searching the wild seas for the *Dolphin*? Or had something worse already happened to them? She forced the thoughts out of her mind as she clutched the railing, fighting to stay on the boat.

Chapter Sixteen

Alex moaned and stirred slightly. The smothering darkness that seemed to blanket her was beginning to lift. Something jagged and very sharp was biting into her shoulder, and her head felt as if it were splitting. One ankle throbbed painfully. She was shivering violently and her clothes—even her tennis shoes—were soaked. She opened her eyes slowly, but everything was spinning around, so she closed them and the darkness swallowed her up once more.

A few minutes later, she opened her eyes again. *Where am I?* she wondered dizzily, shifting so that the rock beneath her no longer bit into her shoulder blade. *What's happened?*

She sat up, clutching her head in dazed bewilderment, trying to remember what had happened. She and Danny had started to explore Kanaha, where huge flocks of gulls and cormorants coexisted peacefully, nesting on the high rocks. But while they were absorbed in watching the birds, a squall had suddenly come up. They had run for the skiff and pushed it out into the sea and started to row as hard as they could toward the spot where the *Dolphin* was anchored. But when they rowed out of the calmer waters of the island and into the battering winds and giant swells of the gale, they had known immediately that they couldn't make it.

"We've got to go back," Danny had shouted. "We'll capsize!"

Where was Danny now? Panic-stricken, Alex looked around. She was sitting on a low ledge of eroded rock, just out of the water. At her feet, the surf foamed and sprayed, drenching her with every wave. The skiff was nowhere in sight. Rain came down in heavy gray sheets. Around her was nothing but rock, not a sign of. . .

Suddenly she caught a glimpse of Danny's sneaker-clad foot, just a few feet away. She cried out, creeping over the rough rocks toward him, pain shooting through her ankle. "Danny! Danny, are you all right?"

He stirred when she reached him. She put her hand on his shoulder and tried to roll him over. A long, bloody cut over his eye was already beginning to crust over, and his shirt was ripped. "Danny," she pleaded, turning his face toward her, "please, wake up, Danny! Say you're okay!"

"Alex?" he moaned thickly. "Alex, is that you?" He opened his eyes and reached out for her, pulling her onto him. "Oh, Alex," he groaned into her neck, his voice choked with rough sobs. "Oh, Alex, you're okay! I thought you were . . ."

Alex wrapped her arms around Danny, and for a long while they lay there, relieved that they were both alive. For a brief moment, Alex thought that she shouldn't be lying there so close to Danny, but the thought disappeared in her relief. She realized, too, that it felt right to have Danny's arms around her.

After a while, Danny sat up, pulling Alex with him. "Are you okay?" he said anxiously. "No bones broken, no cuts?" He explored her face and arms with his fingers.

"No, I'm fine," Alex said. She touched the cut over his eye. "What about you?" There was a puffiness under his eye and the skin was starting to turn green. He'd probably have a black eye in the morning.

"All in one piece," he said grimly. His hair was plastered to his head and his wet shirt stuck to his shoulders. He buried his face in his hands. "Oh, Alex," he said, "I'm so sorry!"

"Sorry!" Alex stared at him.

"Yeah," he said, his voice muffled. "If I'd been watching the weather the way I should have, we'd never have gotten into this fix. And if I'd been smart, I would have figured out that we couldn't make it back to the *Dolphin*. But I panicked, and I . . ." He dropped his hands. "When the boat went over and you flipped out, I figured it was all over. And then when I found you washed up on the rocks unconscious . . ." He shook his head. "Oh, Alex, I thought I'd killed you!"

"But it wasn't *your* fault," Alex cried, putting her arms around him. "I was the one who insisted that we come to the island. It was all my fault. I was the one who . . ."

She stopped. For a minute they stared at each other in surprised silence, and then they broke into crazy laughter.

"I can't believe it," Alex said, when she had gotten control over herself.

"I can't, either," Danny said, wiping the rainwater off his face. "All the time we were together before, we did nothing but compete with each other. And here we are, still at it, competing to see which of us can take the most responsibility for this hare-brained adventure!" He looked up into the gray sky. "And I can't believe that we're sitting here laughing, just after we nearly got wiped out."

Alex sat back. "I can't either," she said, looking into his eyes. "So what do we do now?" She stood up and tried to take a step, but found that she couldn't. "Ouch!" She sat back down on the rocks.

Danny bent down and tenderly probed her swelling ankle with his fingers. "I don't think it's broken," he said. "Looks like a bad sprain." He squinted up at the leaden sky. "It's getting dark, but the wind seems to be easing off some. I'll climb to the top of that rock and see if the water's calm enough for Sean to weigh anchor and motor over here to get us. If it is, I can signal to him. He could never sail in through these rocks. But once the seas die down, he can motor up close enough to use his inflatable raft. We'll be safe on board by suppertime." He started off.

"Wait!" Alex clutched at Danny's arm. "You don't think you're going up there without me, do you?"

"But you can't climb with your ankle like that," Danny said.

"Watch me," Alex said, her tongue between her teeth. "I'm not going to stay by myself. She looked up at him. "Will you help me? Please?"

Danny put an arm around her shoulders. "Lean on me," he commanded, and together they clambered slowly and laboriously up the steep rock to a flat ledge near the top.

"Okay," Danny panted, pulling Alex up over the edge. He turned to look out across the storm-tossed bay. "We should be able to see the *Dolphin* from . . ." His face went white.

"What's wrong?" Alex said. She pulled her legs up and turned, anxious for a sight of the boat. But it wasn't anchored where they had left it! The *Dolphin* was gone!

"Oh, no!" Danny groaned.

"But . . . what could have happened?" Alex cried. "Did it sink? Could it have been driven ashore?" She searched the empty bay with growing horror. There wasn't a sign of the *Dolphin* anywhere.

Danny shook his head slowly. "I don't know," he said. "It . . . it's just gone."

"Could they have sailed away?" Alex asked. She answered her own question with another question. "But why would they sail away and leave us stranded? Unless they thought we were . . ." She swallowed, and her voice dropped to a whisper. "Unless they thought we were drowned."

Danny turned to look at her. His eyes were two deep holes in his face, one rimmed with purple. "Either the *Dolphin* sank in the storm," he said quietly, "or they decided we must have drowned. Maybe they saw the wreckage from the skiff."

"Sank in the storm?" Alex asked in horror, her eyes searching Danny's face. "But Sean is a terrific sailor! How could he . . . ?"

Danny shook his head. "Sean *isn't* that good a sailor, Alex. After we left Los Angeles, I realized that he was afraid of the boat. He's like a little guy with a big dog on a leash, and when he takes it out, the dog takes *him* for a walk. In good weather, he's fine. But when something blows up, he sometimes loses his head. He doesn't think straight. He relies on his crew for a lot of help."

"Relies on his crew?" Alex thought of Kit. "But Kit doesn't know anything about sailing!"

Danny nodded, never taking his eyes off Alex's face. "I think we have to face it, Alex," he said quietly. "Either *they're* dead, or they think *we* are. If they think we're dead, the Coast Guard may eventually come back to search for our bodies. But if *they're* dead . . ." He swallowed hard. "If they're dead, nobody will know where to look for us, Alex."

Alex stared at him for a long time. Then she closed her eyes, the enormity of the situation washing over her like the pounding surf. "What do we do?" she asked, in a small voice.

"There's not much we *can* do right now," Danny said. "It's going to be dark in an hour, and it looks like it's going to rain again. When it does, we'll get even colder." He looked around. "We've got to find shelter."

"The cave," Alex said promptly. "The burial cave."

Danny laughed. "You don't mind sleeping in a burial cave?" he asked.

"I don't think we've got any choice. Where do you suppose it is?"

"My guess is that it's at the highest point on the island," Danny said. He looked at her. "Do you think you can make it?"

"I don't know," Alex admitted. She stopped. How often in her life had she said "I don't know"?

"Well, then, come on," Danny said, holding out his hand. "Let's go before it gets too dark to see what we're doing."

The climb to the top was harder than anything that Alex had ever done. The lava rock crumbled under her fingers and cut into her flesh, and her ankle jabbed with pain every time she bore down on it.

"There must be an easier way," she said breathlessly, when they rested on a ledge. "The natives could never have carried a dead body up here *this* way."

"I'm sure there is," Danny agreed. "There's probably a good path, over on the other side. But we don't have time to hunt for it." He looked at her. "Anyway, we're almost there now."

They reached the cave just as the light began to fade. It seemed to go back quite a distance into the rock, but Alex wasn't inclined to explore it. With a long sigh of relief, she sat down in the shelter of the cave's mouth, while Danny started off to investigate the area around them.

While she waited, Alex gazed out over the sea, hoping against hope for a glimpse of the *Dolphin*. There wasn't a sign of a mast or a sail, no indication of what could have happened to the sailboat. In the other direction, the beach was also deserted, its golden sands a faint glimmer against the darker jungle. Alex pulled her knees up and rested her forehead on them, trying not to give way to panic. What could have happened to Kit? What was going to happen to her and Danny? Although they'd been able to get a drink of rainwater from a hollowed-out depression in the rock, they had no reliable source of water and no food.

It was pitch dark when Danny got back, and Alex was already desperately worried. But when she saw him, her face broke out in a huge smile. "Firewood!" she exclaimed. Danny's arms were filled with splintered wood. "Where did you find firewood?" But then she frowned. What good did it do to have firewood? They didn't have any matches.

Danny grinned. "We were right," he said. "There *is* an easier way down to the sea—a path, as I suspected. And there's another, smaller cave just below us. That's what they must have used as a munitions bunker during the war, because there's a cache of empty boxes. And they're dry enough to burn." He dumped the armload of wood on the rock and fished in his pocket. "And even better"—he held up a square green metal tin—"matches!"

"Matches!" In her excitement, Alex jumped up to fling her arms around him. But the pain in her ankle stabbed at her, and she practically fell into Danny's arms. He grabbed her, laughing.

"Whoa, there," he said. He bent and kissed the tip of her nose. "Let's not celebrate until we see whether they work. After all, these matches have got to be older than we are by at least twenty years."

Alex sat back down on the rock at the mouth of the cave, staring at Danny. It was the second time today he had held her, and she had to admit to herself that even under their present circumstances it had felt wonderful. She shook her head in confusion, fighting the feeling. She couldn't afford to give in, to surrender. Loving cost too much, and she wasn't ready to pay the price all over again.

"Okay," Danny said. "Cross your fingers. Here goes." He struck a match to the neatly crisscrossed stack of wood he had built in the middle of the cave. The first match broke, but the second caught, and after a few minutes the tinder-dry wood caught, and soon a roaring fire was casting eerie shadows on the rough lava walls of the cave. In spite of the fact that they were in Hawaii, the air was crisp and cool, and Alex was glad for the warmth.

"I can't believe it," she sighed, turning to toast the back of her damp shorts in the heat of the fire. "A forty-year-old bonfire."

Stretched out on the floor of the cave next to Alex, Danny chuckled. He had taken off his shirt and draped it over a rock, and the flickering flames gave his skin a warm, golden glow. "Yeah," he said. "I just wish there'd been some forty-year-old hotdogs or marshmallows down there to go with the matches."

Alex looked at him quickly. "Did you look to see?"

"Are you kidding? I went through every box. They were all empty. I thought I was lucky when I found the matches." He sat up and looked at her with concern. "Alex, when I followed the path down to the water, I found something else."

227

She looked at him expectantly.

Danny cleared his throat. "I didn't want to tell you right away. At least until we got warm."

"Why not?" Alex demanded. "Come on, tell."

"It was..." Danny's voice broke and he wiped his forehead with the back of his hand. "Oh, Alex, I wish I didn't have to tell you."

"Danny, what *was* it?" Alex whispered, her eyes fixed on his face. "What did you find?"

"An orange life jacket," Danny said at last, "stamped DOLPHIN."

"Alex closed her eyes. "Oh, no," she whispered. "Does that mean...?" Kit's face rose before her, laughing and gay, her tousled curls bouncing, her eyes sparkling.

"We can't be sure of anything," Danny said. "But it certainly means there's a chance that the *Dolphin* sank during the storm."

They were silent for a while, both staring into the dancing flames. *So much death,* Alex thought, feeling the shadows of the burial cave looming behind her. *How many bodies have been brought up here over the centuries for their final resting place? Will this be my burial place too?*

"I've just thought of something," Alex said finally. She had to swallow before she could go on.

Danny cleared his throat. "Yeah?"

"It's Christmas Eve."

"He stirred the fire. "Yeah," he said. "So it is." After a few minutes, he turned to her and put his fingers under her chin, tipping it toward him, smiling crookedly. "You know something, Alex?" He touched her lips gently with the tip of one finger. "I love you."

Alex kissed his finger. "Yes, I know," she sighed. There might not be another Christmas Eve for them, but at least they had *this* one. Deep inside her, the old feeling stirred, the old love quickened. No matter how much she fought it, she and Danny were joined together in some strange way she didn't understand.

"I love you, too," she said, just before Danny's mouth came down on hers.

Christmas morning dawned bright and clear. Alex woke and stirred stiffly. Her head was still pillowed on Danny's chest, and his arm lay loosely over her. He moved slightly.

"Merry Christmas," Alex said.

"Merry Christmas," Danny replied. He laughed, his arm tightening around her shoulders. "When you go down to the desk to check us out, would you please complain to the management about this mattress? They seem to have substituted rocks for the springs."

Alex laughed and sat up, combing her hair with her fingers. "I'll do that," she said, "while you phone room service and have them send up some breakfast. I'll have six eggs over easy, a pound of hash browns, two loaves of toast, and a half gallon of tomato juice."

With a smile, Danny leaned forward and began to stir the fire. A few embers glowed faintly, and he blew on them until they burst into life. He stood up. "Eggs, madam?" he asked, raising one eyebrow and bowing slightly. "Would that be chicken eggs or cormorant eggs?"

"Cormorant eggs!" Alex leaped up, wincing when she tried to stand on her sore ankle. "Oh, Danny, what a great idea! Maybe we won't starve to death, after all! Where there are birds there *have* to be eggs!"

Danny looped an arm around her shoulders as they went out of the cave and into the bright sunlight. "There's only one hitch," he cautioned. "This is a bird sanctuary and there's a law against raiding the nests. If we're caught, it could mean years in jail."

"Wouldn't it be wonderful to get caught?" Alex asked wistfully. "I'd love to see a park ranger in boots and uniform, blowing his whistle at us after we've raided the nests! I wouldn't even mind telling the judge why . . ."

Suddenly she stopped. "Do you hear that?" she asked. In the distance they could hear the steady roar of a boat motor.

"I hear it!" Danny shouted. He clambered up to the top of the rock and tore off his shirt. "It's the Coast Guard!" he cried, waving his shirt madly. "And they're coming out way!"

"Oh, Danny! Can they see us?" Alex closed her eyes and clenched her fists. For what seemed like forever, Danny stood on the rock, waving his shirt, while the sound of the motor grew louder and louder.

After a few minutes, Danny climbed down off the rock. He came up to Alex and put both hands on her shoulders, his face shining. "They've seen us," he said quietly. "They're coming to pick us up."

"Hooray," Alex whispered. "We're being rescued."

Danny smoothed her hair back from her forehead. "Alex, there's something else," he said.

"Yes?"

"Kit's on board the boat," he said. "Kit's alive! She's brought the Coast Guard, and Elaine and Lori are with her! They've *all* come to rescue us."

Chapter Seventeen

Lori stared at Alex, where she sat with her feet propped on the deck railing, basking in the mid-afternoon sunshine. Alex had just finished telling the harrowing story of her adventure on the island.

"I don't think I could have brought myself to sleep all night in a *burial* cave," Lori said. "Of course, we didn't sleep a wink last night, either. We were so worried about you."

"Right," Elaine said. "When Kit came home without you, we were frantic. The Coast Guard wouldn't go back out at night, so there was nothing we could do."

"I guess I don't understand about Sean," Alex said slowly, turning to Kit. "What happened?"

Kit shook her head. "I don't know," she confessed. "I suppose he just freaked out. He was so afraid that something was going to happen to his dad's boat. And as it turned out, he wasn't a very good sailor, so he was afraid to try anything that seemed risky to him." She laughed. "Boy, what an eye-opener. I mean, he looked so strong and able, but underneath he was just a scared kid."

Alex got up and stretched luxuriously. "I hope nobody minds," she said, "but I think I'm going to go in and take a nap." She laughed. "Last night's accommodations were anything but comfortable."

Elaine stood up, too. "Since we're leaving so early tomorrow," she said, "I'm going down to the beach." She turned to Kit and Lori. "How about joining me? The tide's just going out. We could make one last shell collection."

"I'll come," Kit said eagerly. "I'd like to find a few shells to take back to Glenwood with me, for Justin's family."

"I think I'll stay here," Lori said, glancing at her watch. "Kevin called a little while ago and asked if he could stop by."

Kit arched her eyebrow at Lori. "Sounds serious," she said. "Is it?"

Lori blushed. "Oh, I don't know," she said. She still wasn't sure how she felt about Kevin. He had shown her a wonderful time while she was in Hawaii, but there was something about him she just didn't trust.

The others had been gone for only ten minutes or so when the doorbell rang. It was Kevin, dressed in a pair of striped linen pants with a matching jacket. He was carrying a small round box wrapped in elegant silver paper.

"Merry Christmas, Lori," he said, holding out the package.

"Oh, thank you," Lori managed, feeling both pleased and flustered. She hadn't thought to buy him a gift. She opened the package, being careful not to tear the paper.

"I hope you like it," Kevin said softly, as she lifted the top off the box.

Lori laughed. Inside the box was a plain oyster, its shell looking rough and incongruous in the tissue that surrounded it. "An oyster?" She giggled.

"Why don't you take it out and open it," Kevin suggested, watching her closely.

She took the oyster out of the box and turned it over. She gasped as it opened in her fingers. The oyster was lined with black satin, and on the satin lay a strand of magnificent pearls. Real pearls! They must have cost a fortune!

For a minute she stared at them. "They...they're lovely," she said at last.

"Not as lovely as you," Kevin said. He picked them up and unfastened the silver clasp. "Here. Try them on."

Lori took a step backward. "No," she said,

shaking her head. "I can't."

Kevin frowned. "What do you mean, you can't?"

"They're lovely, Kevin, really they are," Lori said, looking at the pearls in his hand. "But I can't accept an expensive gift like this from you. We've only known each other a few days."

Kevin put the pearls down on the coffee table and stepped toward her. "I know that," he said. He stroked her cheek. "But I want you to think of this as just the beginning. And the pearls as a token of our continuing friendship—and more."

"But I . . ."

"Shh," Kevin said, silencing her with a kiss. "There's so much ahead of us. So many good times, excitement, travel, work."

"Work?" Lori pulled back a little.

Kevin smiled mysteriously. "Yes, work," he said. "Haven't you guessed yet?"

"Guessed what?"

"Guessed who I am."

"Who you *are*?"

Kevin nodded. He stroked her throat with one finger, his eyes following his fingertip. "I'm the head of Cachet's marketing department, Lori."

Lori stood still, stunned. She felt as if he had hit her hard in the stomach, and she could hardly breathe. "Cachet?" she whispered

"I'm sorry I didn't tell you before," he said. "But I *did* drop some hints. I thought you might pick them up and figure it out for yourself."

Then Lori remembered the odd things that Kevin had said the day they drove to the other end of the island. "You're perfect for it," he had said. And there was the fact that he had noticed her lipstick. Of course! It had been Cachet—that's why he'd noticed! She closed her eyes, trying to catch her breath. What a fool she had been to think that he was interested in her for herself! He only wanted to snare her and persuade her to sign the contract.

"I know I should have told you," Kevin said huskily. He bent and kissed her throat. "But I didn't want you to feel that I was putting unfair pressure on you. Clare told me that you weren't sure you wanted the job—although I'm not sure I understand why. But *we're* sure that we want you. *I'm* sure. It's the perfect contract for you, Lori. And you're the perfect model for us." He put his arms around her, pulling her close. "And you're perfect for me," he murmured, his lips against her hair. "I knew it from the minute I saw you. I couldn't resist you. You're so beautiful . . . ."

Lori pulled back, her breath coming in little sobs. "Go away!" she said, her voice breaking.

"What?" Kevin stared at her. "What did you say?"

"I said go away!" Lori shouted. She reached down and scooped up the pearls and threw them at him. "Take your pearls and get out and leave me alone!"

She dashed outside, leaving Kevin standing in the middle of the living room, staring at her with a bewildered look on his face. She ran down the stairs toward the beach, with no destination in mind. She just knew she wanted to be alone. How could he have betrayed her like that! And Clare, too! It had been a setup from the very beginning. Kevin had never been interested in *her*. He had only been interested in her face. *Nobody* ever wanted her for herself. She was only a doll, a mannequin, somebody who looked beautiful and wore clothes elegantly.

But there was more to her than just a face and a figure. Inside her there was intelligence and love and excitement—and pain and hurt and anger, too. But if all anybody ever looked for was a beautiful face, how could she reveal all the *other* things that she was? She stumbled against a piece of driftwood and fell, sobbing, into the warm sand. How could she ever be herself, if all the world wanted was a two-dimensional face on the glossy page of a slick magazine.

Later, she realized that she must have lain there in the sand for almost an hour. Suddenly she felt the touch of a hand on her shoulder, shaking her gently.

"Lori Woodhouse, are you all right?" the old man asked.

Lori sat up in confusion. "I . . . I guess so," she said. She knew that her face was streaked with tears and dirty from lying in the sand. She rubbed her eyes with the backs of her hands and brushed the sand off her cheeks. "I guess I fell asleep," she said. *I cried myself to sleep,* she thought. *I haven't done that since I was eight years old.*

The old man bent over and touched her smudged cheek with his finger. The look in his eyes was soft and knowing. "Are you thirsty?" he asked. "Would you like to come home with me and share a cup of tea?"

Lori wasn't even tempted to say no. Instinctively, she knew that no matter how shabby the old man looked or how poor he might be, he was still a friend, and she could trust him. She felt very much in need of friendship just then, so she got to her feet and followed him up the beach until they came to a flight of wooden stairs almost obscured by a cascade of tropical plants.

The stairs led at an angle up the hill and then out onto a wide wooden deck that jutted out of the trees, hidden under a shady canopy of breadfruit trees. The deck was tastefully decorated with Oriental sculptures and pieces of art. From somewhere close by came the musical tinkling of wind chimes and the tranquil rippling of a fountain. On the far side of the deck, shoji-screen doors were open, showing a view of a lovely Japanese-style home.

Lori blinked. Perhaps this was a shortcut to the old man's shack. Were they trespassing? She waited for someone to come out of the house and order them away.

"Ono?" the old man called. He clapped his hands. Through the shoji doors came a small, stooped man wearing a Japanese kimono. He bowed low. "Sir?" he asked respectfully.

"There will be two for tea, Ono." The old man turned to Lori. "Do you like jasmine tea, my dear?" he asked.

Speechless, Lori nodded. *This* was his house? Judging from his appearance, she had thought that . . . She stopped. She had been lying on the sand, weeping hysterically because Kevin and Clare had only been willing to see as far as her face. What gave *her* the ability or the right to judge the old man on the basis of his clothes and the way he wore his hair? Kevin and Clare were wrong—but she had been just as wrong. She had made exactly the kind of judgment they had made.

"Would you like to see the house, Lori?" the man asked. He smiled, and his blue eyes twinkled. "There are some things that I want you to see."

Lori gulped. "Yes," she said. "Please."

She followed him inside, and when he bent to take off his shoes, she took hers off too. He handed her a pair of little felt slippers. "It's Ono's idea, actually," he said, dropping his voice into a conspiratorial whisper. "It's something they do in Japan, and I like to keep him happy. He's such a dear friend, and he's been with me for a very long time."

Lori put on the slippers, noticing that the elegant inlaid wooden floors gleamed without a trace of dust. She turned and looked around her. The house was decorated in an Oriental style, with low furniture, subdued lighting, and beautiful flower arrangements placed in surprising nooks and crannies. The windows had no curtains or drapes, and each one seemed to open out onto its own private garden.

Lori went to one and looked out at a tiny goldfish pond, which was set into a bed of glistening white sand, raked in a delicate swirl. One lovely fern hung over the pool, and a stone sculpture of a dignified frog, green with moss, sat on the edge.

"Ah, so you like Ono's little window surprises," the old man said, coming up behind her.

"It's lovely," Lori said. She turned and surveyed the quiet, peaceful room. Its utter simplicity made Clare Karlysle's condo, in contrast, seem gauche and overdone.

After a minute, the man held out his hand. "Come along," he said gently. "I have another surprise for you."

Together, they walked through the house, the old man pushing aside the rice-paper screens that separated the rooms. Each room seemed to Lori more beautiful than the one before, each filled with lovely pieces of art, jade carvings, ancient stone Buddhas with inscrutable smiles. In one, leaning against the wall, she saw the walking stick the old man had used on the beach the other day. Here, she could see that it, too, was a work of art.

But it was the photographs that caught Lori's eye. They hung in every room, all were black-and-white, most of them framed very simply. But one room, which seemed to be a gallery, was filled with nothing but photographs, together with a few other pieces of art. Some of the photographs were of abstract forms, some of the beach and the ocean, others of works of art, still others of people. In one, she recognized the outlines of the sand-sculpture dunes where she had met the old man.

She paused in front of the photograph. It was small, but it captured the massiveness of the dune shape and the power of the wind that had carved it. It captured the wild, desolate feeling of the place. She sighed. If only *she* could capture that feeling in her drawing. If she had that kind of skill, she would know what to do with her life. The photograph was signed. She bent over, recognizing the name from one of her art classes back at Glenwood. Robert Stillman. Robert Stillman was one of the best photographers in America — perhaps the very best, her art teacher had said. He didn't do a great deal of work, but the work he did was of extraordinarily high quality.

"Do you like that one?" the man asked.

"Oh, I do," Lori replied, her eyes fixed on it.

Carefully, the man took it down from the wall. "Then I'd like to give it to you," he said, holding it out. "Merry Christmas, Lori."

"Oh, but I can't," Lori said. For the second time today, she'd been offered a gift she couldn't accept. "It . . . it's far too valuable."

"That's why I'm giving it to you."

Lori stared at him, her eyes growing rounder. Suddenly his face seemed very familiar. She was sure she'd seen a picture of him somewhere. She swallowed.

"Yes, that's right." The old man nodded gently. "I'm Robert Stillman." He smiled. "That's why I can give you this photograph, you see. It will be a reminder to you of the time we talked together in the dunes." He held it out to her again, and this time Lori took it. "Do you remember what I said to you that day?" Mr. Stillman asked.

"Some of it," she said, in a small voice.

"I told you two things," Mr. Stillman said, leading her into a little garden off the gallery. There was a fountain there, and from somewhere nearby came the sound of Oriental music. A single tall bamboo plant cast a lacy shadow on a rice-paper screen. Ono came out, bearing a tray with a pot of tea and two jewel-like *raku* cups. He poured the tea carefully and handed Lori her cup.

"I told you that you were a talented artist," Mr. Stillman said, watching Lori sip her tea. It was sweet and very fragrant, like jasmine blossoms. "But you couldn't believe what I said because you thought I was just an old beachcomber, probably a little forgetful and certainly no student of the arts." He smiled gently. "Am I right?"

Lori nodded. That was exactly what she had thought.

Mr. Stillman picked up his own cup. "Well, I'll tell you again that you have talent. It is not well developed, but it is certainly there. Now do you believe me?"

Uncertainly, Lori nodded. She couldn't imagine that a man of Mr. Stillman's reputation would lie to her. "I believe you," she said softly.

"Good." Mr. Stillman exclaimed. "I also think that you should develop your artistic talent, that you should study and practice and see whether you have the dedication that it takes to be a real artist."

Lori put down her cup. "But how can I do that," she burst out, "if I have to be a model? I mean, I have to make a living. My parents can't support me in art school."

"I told you two things that day," Mr. Stillman went on. "I also told you that you have a beautiful face. Do you remember?"

Lori nodded again. He *had* told her that. Somehow, it hadn't seemed quite so *empty* as when Kevin said it.

Mr. Stillman turned and gestured. "Look."

Lori looked where he pointed. There was a photograph hanging just inside the door of the gallery, but she could see it very clearly from where she sat. It was the profile of a beautiful Hawaiian woman, looking out to sea.

"That woman is also very beautiful," Mr. Stillman said. "Like you. And like you, she has an inner beauty, a beauty of spirit that shines in her eyes, that finds its expression in the lines of her mouth and the turn of her head. It is that inner beauty that you see when you look at that photograph, because that is what *I* saw as I stood behind the camera. That is what you can show to the camera when you model—not only the outer person, but the inner person as well." He turned to Lori. "I would like to photograph you, Lori," he said.

For a moment, Lori couldn't believe she had heard him correctly. Robert Stillman was asking *her* to sit for him?

"I'm coming to New York for a show next month. I have a studio there. If you would work with me for a few days, I'll be glad to pay you for your time. And I'll take you to meet the director of the Art Institute and offer my personal recommendation for your admission."

Suddenly, tears came to Lori's eyes. "You would do all this," she asked, "for a girl you met on the beach?"

"I would do all this," Mr. Stillman said

quietly, "for a fellow artist. And for a woman whose spirit is as beautiful as her face."

Lori couldn't help herself. She broke down and wept, while Mr. Stillman gently patted her hand.

Chapter Eighteen

"Don't forget your sweater," Elaine reminded Kit. "It's hanging in the kitchen."

It was Christmas night, and both bedrooms
of the condo were littered with clothes and
suitcases and makeup kits, as the girls got
ready to pack up for home. Tomorrow they
would drive the rental car back to Kahului,
catch an Aloha Airlines flight back to Honolulu, and then catch their flights home. Elaine was going back to San Francisco, and Kit
was flying with her. The two of them would
drive down to Glenwood together, where Kit
was planning to spend the rest of the holiday
with Justin.

"Here's your toothpaste," Alex told Kit. "I
don't know how it got in my bathroom." She
sat down on the bed and looked around at the
clothes and souvenirs scattered across the
room. "Do you think we'll be able to get all of
this back into the suitcases?"

Elaine laughed. "I'm not so worried about repacking the stuff that I brought," she said. "It's the stuff that I *bought* that I'm worried about. And the stuff that I found on the beach." She surveyed the heap of sandy shells and pieces of driftwood at the foot of the bed, and then picked up a dozen in her arms and went into the bathroom to rinse them off in the bathtub.

"Hey, wait," Alex said. "I want to ask you something."

Elaine put her load of shells in the bathtub and went back for more. "Yeah?" she asked. She had a sneaking suspicion she knew what Alex was going to ask. "What is it?"

Alex looked at her with interest. "I want to know what happened with Joe. Here it is, almost twenty-four hours later, and you haven't said a word about what happened. Did you go to his apartment?"

Elaine smiled. "Are you sure you *really* want to know?" she asked.

Kit straightened up from her suitcase. "I *do*," she said. "I want to hear every detail."

Lori appeared at the door with a smile on her face. "Did I hear that Elaine was going to tell us about her fling?"

Elaine threw up her hands and sat down on the floor next to her shells. "You guys," she said affectionately. "You haven't changed a bit, have you? Still as nosy as ever."

"Well, maybe we are being nosy, but this is *important*," Kit insisted. "I mean, you painted this wonderful picture of Joe and the no-strings-attached fling that you were going to have."

"And now we're expecting a really juicy confession," Alex added. She curled up her feet and waited expectantly. "So confess."

Elaine picked up a perfectly fluted pink shell with a delicate gold edge. She planned to give it to Andrea to keep on her windowsill. "There's nothing to confess," she said.

"Oh, come on," Kit hooted. "After the big buildup you gave us, do you expect us to believe that *nothing* happened?"

Elaine glanced around. Kit was shaking her head, and Alex and Lori were both staring at her with disbelieving looks.

"Well, maybe Elaine just doesn't want to tell us," Lori said finally. "I mean, if she wants to keep it private, we shouldn't . . ."

"There's nothing to keep private," Elaine confessed sheepishly. "Honest."

"Nothing?" the girls all asked.

Elaine nodded. She put down the shell. "I went to Joe's apartment. And yes, he wanted more than just a few kisses. At first, I thought that's what I wanted, too." She sighed, remembering. "I mean, he really *is* gorgeous.

And he's nice, too, underneath it all. But I just don't love him."

"So love really mattered, after all," Alex said softly, thinking of Danny and of her plans to fly to California to be with him over spring break.

Elaine picked up a pair of identical conch shells that she had found for the twins and held them to her ears. In the distance, she could hear the surf roaring, and she thought of the wonderfully free feeling of bodysurfing across the face of the wave. She nodded in answer to Alex's question. "I kept telling myself that love doesn't necessarily count when you're having a fling," she said, putting down the shells. "But when it came right down to it, I found out that wasn't true. And I guess I found out that there's no such thing as the perfect fling, because there's something really important that's missing from one."

Kit cleared her throat. "Well, now that Elaine's confessed, I guess it's time for me to confess what I've decided about Justin."

Elaine turned to look at Kit. She had closed her suitcase and was sitting on top of it, her chin in her hands. Her hair was mussed up, and there was a smudge at the corner of her mouth. Her big blue eyes looked very serious.

"Well, shall we get ready to send engagement presents?" Elaine asked.

Kit shook her head. "No engagement, no engagement presents." She held up her hand, her eyes shining. "Oh, it's not that I don't love Justin. I do! In fact, meeting Sean O'Donnell and getting to know him reminded me just how important and wonderful Justin is in my life. But I have this feeling that it's not time yet for us to get engaged."

Alex frowned. "How do you think Justin is going to respond? Don't you think he'll be angry?"

Kit smiled. "Well, maybe a little, at first," she said. "But I have a feeling that he'll understand—once I get through explaining it to him."

Elaine got up and went to the door that led onto the deck. The sun had set, but the sky was a soft, translucent shade of pink, reflected radiantly in the ocean. It reminded her of the night they had come, bringing with them their expectations of wonderful adventure, their problems to solve and lessons to learn. The week had been very different from what they had imagined. Alex had nearly drowned, Kit had decided not to get engaged, Lori had found a new way of thinking about herself and her modeling work, and *she* had found out that love had to be at the heart of things.

She turned back to the group. "Let's go for

251

a walk on the beach," she said quietly. "That's the perfect place to say 'aloha.'"

As they walked together down the sand, under the full moon that shimmered above the tropical forest, Elaine knew that indeed love *was* at the heart of things. Love and friendship.

After a while, they all joined hands and looked out at the sea. The night was very quiet, but in the distance they could hear the faint sound of Hawaiian guitars coming from the direction of the hotel. They all hummed along, softly. Tomorrow, it would be time to say good-bye. They didn't know when they would be together again, but they knew that as long as they lived, they would never forget the wonderful week they had spent together, their special Hawaiian Christmas.